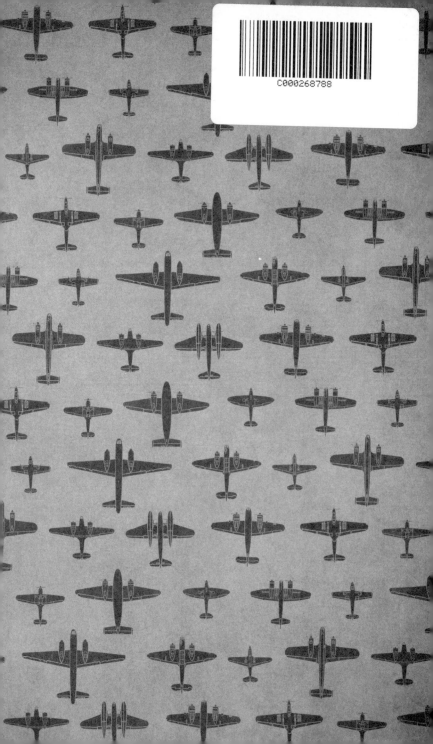

Biggles: The Second Case

William Earl Johns was an English adventure writer, best known as the creator of the beloved Biggles stories, which drew on his experience as a pilot in the First World War. After his flying career with the RAF, Johns became a newspaper air correspondent, an occupation he combined with editing and illustrating books about flying. He wrote over 160 books, including nearly 100 Biggles titles.

Also by Captain W. E. Johns and published by Canelo

Biggles' WW2 Adventures

Biggles in the Baltic
Biggles Sees It Through
Biggles in Borneo

Biggles Between the Wars

Biggles Flies North
Biggles, Secret Agent
Biggles in the Jungle

Biggles, Special Air Detective

Sergeant Bigglesworth, CID
Biggles: The Second Case
Biggles on the Hunt
Biggles Takes a Holiday
Biggles Breaks the Silence

BIGGLES

The SECOND CASE

CAPT · W · E · JOHNS

CANELO

First published in the United Kingdom in 1948 by Hodder and Stoughton
as *Biggles' Second Case*

This edition published in the United Kingdom in 2023 by

Canelo
Unit 9, 5th Floor
Cargo Works, 1–2 Hatfields
London SE1 9PG
United Kingdom

A CIP catalogue record for this book is available from the British Library.

Print ISBN 978 1 80436 442 0
Ebook ISBN 978 1 80032 937 9

Look for more great books at www.canelo.co

Printed and bound in Great Britain by Clays Ltd, Elcograf S.p.A.

1

This book contains views and language on nationality, sexual politics, ethnicity, and society which are a product of the time in which the book is set. The publisher does not endorse or support these views. They have been retained in order to preserve the integrity of the text.

CHAPTER I

Aftermath of War

Constable 'Ginger' Hebblethwaite, of the Scotland Yard Air Squad, regarded the other three members of his division with moody disfavour. They were Sergeant Bigglesworth, D.S.O., D.F.C., and Constables Algy Lacey and Lord Bertie Lissie, all of whom had left the Royal Air Force to form the nucleus of a flying unit attached to the Criminal Investigation Department. It should be stated that Lord Lissie had for so long refrained from using his title that he had almost forgotten that he was a peer of the realm.

'What I say is this,' remarked Ginger, with gloomy emphasis, 'if Raymond can't find something better for us to do than sit here working out schemes to provide policemen with wings, schemes that are always turned down by the Treasury on account of expense, it's time we asked for our discharges and went off on our own.'

'Where?' asked Biggles.

'Anywhere,' retorted Ginger vaguely, waving a hand in the direction of the window, presumably to indicate the blue sky.

'Doing what?' inquired Biggles.

Ginger hesitated. 'Anything,' he retorted, still more vaguely. 'I want action,' he went on, warming to his subject. 'I wasn't cut out for the Chairborne Division. In six months we've had one case.' A note of bitterness crept into his voice. 'What's wrong with our crooks? Have they lost their nerve or something? The miserable truth is, they're not so snappy at getting into the atmosphere as Raymond expected they would be.'

Biggles frowned. 'I don't know that I approve of the familiar way you refer to the Assistant Commissioner of Police, and an Air Commodore at that, by his bare surname, as if he were a sort of lackey. There's something in what you say, I'll admit, but *he* can't help it if the best crooks continue to travel on wheels, or on the soles of their feet.'

'While they do that we shall just sit here and wear out the seats of our pants to no purpose,' growled Ginger.

'All right. Our appointment was only temporary so there is nothing to prevent us from asking for our discharge tickets when we feel we've had enough of doing nothing. I don't like it any more than you do. As a matter of fact, I spoke to the Air Commodore about it only yesterday. He said he'd try to find us a good line in crooks if we'd hang on a bit longer.'

Ginger shrugged. 'Okay. Tell him to get busy. This messing about an office waiting for an enterprising crook to take flight isn't my idea of a gay life.'

Biggles took a cigarette from his case, tapped it on the back of his hand and looked at Algy and Bertie in turn. 'How do you fellows feel about it?'

'Frankly, I'm getting a trifle browned-off,' admitted Algy. 'This is a nice little office, as offices go, but rooms always did give me a sort of shut-up feeling. I need air;

and I like to be able to move without bumping into something.'

'Same here, old boy – absolutely,' declared Bertie. 'The fug of the central heating in this bally mausoleum is slowly choking me to death – if you see what I mean? Give me the jolly old wide open spaces every time – yes, by Jove!'

The door opened and Air Commodore Raymond stepped into the room. 'Did I hear someone talking about wide open spaces?' he inquired.

'You did, sir,' answered Biggles. 'I'm afraid there's mutiny brewing here. Apparently Scotland Yard isn't big enough to house these skylarks.' He indicated the others with a jab of his thumb. 'They were just remarking that if they don't soon stretch their wings their feathers will start to drop off.'

The Air Commodore smiled. 'In that case I shall have to do something about it,' he announced. 'As a matter of fact, I came here to discuss this very thing. Talking of spaces, I have in mind a space so wide that no one – as far as I know – has ever got to the other side of it. As for fresh air – why, they can have a million square miles of it all to themselves.'

Bertie opened his eyes so wide that his monocle fell out. But he caught it deftly. 'Really? By Jove! That's marvellous, sir – absolutely marvellous.'

'Come down to my office and I'll show you what I mean,' invited the Air Commodore.

They all followed the Air Commodore to his private office where they were requested to be seated. Only the Air Commodore remained standing, and he took up a position – in the manner of a schoolmaster – in front of a large-scale Admiralty chart that had been fastened to the wall.

'Now, gentlemen,' he resumed. 'We have before us a case that should provide you not only with those things for which you are pining, but provide them in quantities sufficient to satisfy even *your* extravagant requirements. The problem is not precisely the one for which you were originally enlisted into the air branch of the C.I.D., because, for one thing, the men against whom you will be opposed are outside the jurisdiction of the Yard. The matter is largely political, as opposed to criminal. Your opponents have as yet committed no actual crime in, or against, this country, although there is every expectation that they will unless we take steps to prevent it. Further, they are not airmen. They do not – as far as we know – possess an aircraft. They may never fly. Nevertheless, the case is one in which we on our side might with great advantage employ aircraft. Indeed, the time at our disposal is so limited that no other vehicle would be of the slightest use. Make yourselves comfortable while I run over the summary of evidence. It will take a little while.'

There was a pause while chairs were drawn closer to the chart.

'The story opened during the latter part of the war,' continued the Air Commodore. 'The U-boat had been beaten in the Atlantic and our lines of communication with the Empire were running pretty well; nevertheless, a number of ships disappeared, in rather mysterious circumstances. They vanished. There were no survivors. Until recently there was not the slightest indication of what happened to them. Curiously enough, all these ships were

4

lost in the same area; that is to say, within a few hundred miles of each other. The area concerned was the South Indian Ocean. The ships were on the Grand Circle route between West Australia and the Cape of Good Hope. Now it happened that these ships were important – or four of them were. They carried a considerable quantity of bullion, gold which had been mined in Australia and was on its way to Great Britain. When I tell you that the value of this gold was in the order of five million pounds sterling you will perceive that we are dealing with what the Prime Minister might call a sum of money of the first order. Naturally, the Bank of England and the Admiralty supposed this money to be at the bottom of the sea, beyond hope of recovery, but evidence has just reached us which suggests that they may be wrong. And the manner in which this evidence was brought to light was, to say the least of it, dramatic.' The Air Commodore paused while he picked up a long ruler that lay on his desk.

'A week ago today, a man, a German, reported himself at British Headquarters in Germany, and asked for an interview with the Commander-in-Chief, the reason given being that he had important information to impart. There was a delay. While the visitor stood in the vestibule, waiting, another man entered. This man, too, we presume, was a German. Without the slightest warning of what he intended, he drew a revolver from his pocket and fired three bullets at point-blank range into the body of the man who stood there waiting. Having done that he bolted, shooting down a civilian who tried to intercept him. The assassin, I am sorry to say, got clear away, but unfortunately for him, and fortunately for us, as it turned

5

out, the victim of the attack was not dead. He died later, but before he died he made an astonishing statement. Admittedly, it was supported by no proof, but considered in connection with what we know to be fact there is sound reason for thinking that the man told the truth. A dying man has no reason to lie, anyway. And now, here, briefly, is the statement of the man who was shot – as it was hoped, to seal his lips for ever.' The Air Commodore picked up several sheets of foolscap paper pinned together at the corners.

'The name of the murdered man is common enough in Germany. It was Muller. During the war he had been a sailor in the German Navy, serving for three years in U-boats. His final appointment was in the U-517, under the command of Captain Ulrich von Schonbeck. The Admiralty know all about von Schonbeck. He was a typical specimen of a hard-boiled Prussian Nazi – efficient, ruthless, and a fanatical admirer of Hitler. According to Muller, von Schonbeck was specially chosen for an assignment of unusual importance. It was this. In their pre-war preparations for a world war the Germans had established over the Seven Seas a number of secret U-boat bases. At the moment we are concerned only with one of them. It was on an unknown island in the South Indian Ocean. I'll come back to this *unknown* aspect of the island in a minute. Von Schonbeck's job was to get to this base and from it attack our ships that were operating between West Australia and South Africa. Actually, he was to do more than attack these ships. He was to seize the gold they were carrying, gold that would enable the Nazi leaders to buy badly needed commodities from neutral countries. It must be conceded that von Schonbeck did his job well. He got away with five million pounds' worth. With that we have no quarrel. It was all part of the grim business of war. But it seems that in order to cover his traces he not only sent every ship which he intercepted to the bottom – he murdered in cold blood every man, woman and child aboard them. You must understand that some of these ships were steamers carrying passengers. If Muller is to be believed – and as I have said, there is no reason to suppose he lied – von Schonbeck's usual method was this. He would stop a ship and order the crew and the passengers into the boats – having stated his intention of sinking the ship. He would then take the gold and sink the ship. This done, he would turn the U-boat's machine-guns on the helpless life-boats – with what result it is easy to imagine.'

'Swine,' muttered Biggles.

The Air Commodore ignored the interruption. 'In this foul work Muller admitted that he had taken a hand, acting under orders which he dare not disobey. It now becomes easy to understand why these ships disappeared leaving no trace behind them. Very well. It was too far, and too risky, for von Schonbeck to come home after each sinking, so the gold was stored at his island base, pending instructions from Germany.

'That was the position when the war ended. Von Schonbeck was still in the South Indian Ocean with the loot of his many raids safely tucked away. He had no intention of handing the gold back to us. With the Navy on the watch for him he dare not even risk trying to get it home. So he did what so many pirates have done. He buried it, and with an empty U-boat made his way back to Germany to find out what was happening. He

7

didn't hurry. He prowled home in easy stages. In fact, he was so long getting home that the U-517 was posted as missing, presumed lost. Another reason for the delay was this. Von Schonbeck, instead of proceeding to the nearest port, as he should have done, made his way to one of the small German islands in the Baltic. Leaving the submarine hidden, with the crew still on board, he went to Berlin to reveal the existence of the gold to the surviving leaders of the Nazi party. At least, that's what he told the crew, and it may have been true. Apparently he failed to make contact with his Nazi friends, and finding himself with five million pounds' worth of gold which nobody knew anything about, he conceived the bright idea of keeping it for himself – or so we may presume. As a proposition it must have looked not only attractive, but simple. Into this plot, on his return to the U-boat, he took his first lieutenant, a brutal fellow named Thom. They still had the U-boat, remember, and the idea now was that they should return to the island, collect the gold, refit and refuel from the secret stores and then go on to a creek in the Magellan Straits. From here the gold could be transported by easy stages up South America to a small town in Chile, where there was still a large German colony. Von Schonbeck, Thom, and the crew, could then live in luxury for the rest of their days.

'That was the plan as it was put to the crew. The crew had to be told, of course, as they would be needed to man the U-boat. We now come to the first snag in this pretty scheme. Not all the men wanted to go. The murdered man, Muller, now comes into the picture. According to his dying statement, five men, of whom he was one, had had enough of the sea. Three were married and were anxious to get home to their families. Apart from that it seems that these men did not altogether trust von Schonbeck and Thom. Having seen something of their unscrupulous methods it seemed to these men that Von Schonbeck, rather than share the loot, would be just as likely to bump them off when he had no more use for them. But the point is this. Von Schonbeck, having told the crew what he intended, now found himself in a quandary. If he allowed these five men to go it seemed not unlikely that they, or one of them, would sooner or later spill the beans – perhaps sell the information to us. But it did not come to that. Von Schonbeck took jolly good care it didn't. The suspicions of the five men who refused to go were well founded. Von Schonbeck and Thom, aided by the rest of the crew, shot them in cold blood and threw their bodies into the sea. Now, had all these men been dead we should have known nothing of this; but for once von Schonbeck's brutal efficiency let him down. Muller, although wounded, was still alive, but unconscious. The cold water revived him, and with the help of the tide he was able to reach the nearby shore. But he must have been seen, or else some peasants who befriended him unwittingly betrayed him. About that we don't know. Muller didn't know. All we know is, Thom was soon on his track. Unfortunately, Muller was unaware of it. He made his way to Berlin, and burning for revenge after the foul attempt to murder him, as soon as he was able he went to our people with the object of betraying the plot. You can guess the rest. Thom, still on his track, caught up with him while he was waiting for an interview at General Headquarters. Thom shot Muller, got away, and no doubt made straight back for the U-boat. Muller, this time mortally wounded, only lived long enough to tell us the story I have just told to you. By this time no doubt the U-517 is on its way to get the gold.'

CHAPTER II

Biggles Asks Some Questions

'If I may interrupt, I'd like to be a little more clear on that point,' put in Biggles. 'Are you sure the U-boat has headed back for the Indian Ocean.'

'Not absolutely sure,' admitted the Air Commodore. 'Muller gave us the name of the island in the Baltic where the submarine had hidden herself, and we weren't long getting to it; but by the time we were on the spot she had gone. Of course, there is just a chance that von Schonbeck is still lying low somewhere in the Baltic, but if the vessel has gone, and it certainly has gone, it seems far more likely that it is on its way to its South Indian base. I can think of no reason why von Schonbeck should delay putting his plan into operation – can you?'

'No,' admitted Biggles. 'If the U-517 has got clear of the North Sea, then von Schonbeck looks like getting away with it.'

'If our judgment of the situation is correct the U-517 has been on its way for a fortnight,' said the Air Commodore. 'Muller was unconscious for some days; we had to wait for him to come round to learn what it was all about. Von Schonbeck had plenty of time to slip away. But there is one thing he does not know. He doesn't know that we are wise to his scheme. He doesn't know that Muller talked. He thinks Muller was shot dead by Thom – that he died instantly.'

'How can you say what von Schonbeck thinks?' asked Biggles quickly.

A ghost of a smile softened the Air Commodore's austere features. 'Our intelligence people are good at dealing with situations of this sort,' he said dryly. 'They issued a story of the shooting for the Press. It was not exactly true, in that it asserted that the man murdered at British Headquarters had died without opening his lips. His name, and that of his assailant, were unknown. The motive of the crime was, therefore, a mystery. That was the story we put out in the newspapers. Thom would certainly see a newspaper because a criminal always makes a point of reading the Press notices of his crime, in the hope of learning how much the police know, or what they think. Thom would show the paper to von Schonbeck, and we can imagine the two scoundrels patting each other on the back at their astute handling of the situation. No word of the truth has been allowed to leak out, so von Schonbeck and his crew of cutthroats must believe that they are now safe from pursuit. That is about the only trump card that we hold.'

'The Navy has been looking for the U-517, I presume?' queried Biggles.

'Of course. So have Coastal Command and the Fleet Air Arm. But von Schonbeck must be an expert at dodging anti-submarine patrols or he would not have lived as long as he has. He's a wily bird. We haven't seen a sign of him.'

Biggles frowned. 'But we ought to be able to catch him.'

The Air Commodore shook his head dubiously. 'I should like to think so. But we are up against a big snag. We don't know the name of the island for which the U-boat is making – the island where the gold is hidden.'

Biggles looked surprised. 'But surely Muller told you the name of the island?'

'He did not, for the simple reason he didn't know the name of it himself. It was always referred to by von Schonbeck as The Island. That's what I meant when I described it a moment ago as an unknown island. In fact, incredible though it may seem, the island may not have a name. It may not be shown on Admiralty charts.'

Biggles's eyes opened wide in astonishment. 'Is that possible?'

'Easily. Perhaps we had better have a word or two about islands. In your study of Admiralty charts you must have noticed, scattered about the oceans, tiny specks against which occur the letters, E.D.?'

'I always understood they meant, Existence Doubtful.'

'Quite right,' confirmed the Air Commodore. 'These are mostly islands which have been reported as having been sighted by ships' captains, but could not afterwards be found by Admiralty survey ships or other craft. Unfortunately for us, the South Indian Ocean is particularly rich in such islands. I have been over at the Admiralty making inquiries about some of them.' The Air Commodore picked up some slips of paper that lay on his desk.

'For example, there is Swain Island,' he resumed. 'It was first reported by Captain Swain in 1800. He did not land. Several ships have seen the island since, and yet, absurd though it must seem in these days of swift transport, we still don't know where it is. In 1830 a Captain Gardner fixed the position of Swain Island, yet when two of our survey ships went out it was not to be found. In 1841 Captain Dougherty passed the island at three hundred yards and kept it in sight all day. He has described it in some detail. Later it was seen by a Captain Keates. It was seen in 1885, 1886 and 1890. In 1893 a Captain White sailed round it and reported it to be eight miles long and eighty feet high. No one has seen it since. Every attempt to find it has failed. In recent years Captain Scott, the famous Antarctic explorer, sailed over the spot and reported soundings of three miles! As late as 1932 the Admiralty erased the island from its charts; but it is hard to believe that all those captains could have been wrong. Yet where *is* the island? We don't know. Nobody knows – except possibly von Schonbeck, if it happens to be his secret base. Unfortunately Swain Island is not an isolated case. There are several islands that seem to be playing this glorified game of hide-and-seek, so you see how complicated becomes our quest for this slippery Nazi and his U-boat? Take the Auroras. Here we have a group of islands playing the same game. They were first reported in 1762. And the Royal Company Islands which, having been on our charts for years, were removed by the Admiralty in 1904 because no one could find them. But let's not waste time on islands that may or may not exist. The story of one is the story of all the others. Let's consider South Indian Ocean islands that *do* exist. They alone are enough to give us a headache, for there are plenty of them scattered over a few million square miles of ocean. They are all uninhabited. Some have not been visited for thirty or forty years. In fact, there are very few people alive who have seen them, let alone landed. Any one of them might be von Schonbeck's island.' The Air Commodore indicated a spot with his long pointer.

'First, there are the Crozets,' he went on. 'It's quite a big group. The largest is Possession Island. Then we have St. Paul Island, Prince Edward Island, Macdonald Island and the Heard Islands. Here we have Penguin Island, a sheer rock rising a thousand feet out of the sea which has never been landed on. Here we have Hog Island, Inaccessible Island, Earl Island.' The Air Commodore moved his pointer. 'Over here we have the Apostle group, two large islands and ten smaller ones. I must tell you that some of these islands are the peaks of extinct volcanoes – and not so very long extinct, either. They hold boiling springs. If you stir the ground it smokes, reeking of sulphur. On the other hand, some of the islands are of considerable size. Kerguelen Island, for instance, is forty-five miles long by eight miles wide.'

'And do you mean to say, sir, that no one lives on an island of that size?' Ginger asked.

'I do. The chief trouble is, there is no communication with anywhere. Kerguelen is two thousand one hundred miles from the nearest inhabited land. Who's going to live on a place like that? One might as well live on the moon. Fancy having toothache, and the nearest dentist over two thousand miles away! Then again, these islands are not the voluptuous desert islands of romantic fiction. They are bleak, cold, inhospitable, treeless. None has been fully explored. There are quicksands to contend with – glaciers, torrents, roaring waterfalls. Deep fiords cut into them as they do into the coast of Norway. On ninety-nine days out of a hundred the wind comes screaming across thousands of miles of ocean to vent its fury on its first obstruction.'

'Then nothing lives on these beastly islands – what?' murmured Bertie.

'Oh, yes. There is quite a lot of wild life – sea-birds, seals, penguins. There are rabbits, wild hogs and wildcats, descendants of domestic animals left behind at some time or other by passing ships. It must be possible to live on at least some of these islands, though, for in 1821 the survivors of a ship named *The Princess of Wales* were on the Crozets for two years before being picked up. As far as the Admiralty is aware the last visit to the Crozets was in 1901. This is what Admiralty Sailing Directions have to say about Kerguelen.'

> Notwithstanding its natural defects and desolate character it is not without value. It has safe and commodious harbours and an abundance of fresh water. Kerguelen has never been explored, the boggy nature of the interior making this extremely difficult. The western coast is under the constant bombardment of gales and high seas.

The Air Commodore tossed the paper he held on to his desk. 'Well, there it is. Von Schonbeck is undoubtedly making for one of these islands, on which he has hidden a treasure worth five million pounds. But from what I have said you will have gathered a rough idea of what sort of job you will have to find him.'

Biggles smiled wanly. 'I was wondering when you were coming to that.'

The Air Commodore laughed. 'You didn't suppose that I was giving you a lecture on islands merely to pass the time, did you?'

Biggles shook his head. 'No, sir. But why pick on us? I mean, how does the Yard come into the affair? I should have thought the matter was one for the services – the Navy or the Air Force – to handle.'

'In a way it is,' admitted the Air Commodore. 'But the thing is one of those complicated affairs that occur from time to time. Strictly speaking, the rounding up of the U-517, of all U-boats, is the Navy's business. From the criminal angle, the shooting of Muller and the civilian who tried to stop Thom, the matter is one for the German police. Situated as they are there is little they can do, so they have asked for our co-operation. Then there is the question of the gold. It was heavily insured, and the companies concerned came to us, the proper civil authority, to protect their interests. We automatically watch the political side. As a result of this, to prevent overlapping, the Government has put the investigation into the hands of the Yard, with power to call on the fighting services should they be required. We have in fact invited the Navy and the Air Force to co-operate by calling on them for assistance. So far they have failed to achieve any result. Now, I'm afraid, ships are out of it. If von Schonbeck has slipped through the cordon which the Admiralty threw from the English Channel to the Shetlands, and it begins to look as though he has, he must be well on his way. What course he will take on reaching the Atlantic we don't know, and it would be futile to guess. What we do know is that his objective is in the South Indian Ocean. But, as you will see from the map, that particular ocean

17

covers a large portion of the earth's surface. To search millions of square miles of open water by surface-craft, for one solitary U-boat, would take years. Our only hope of covering such a vast area is by employing aircraft, and that is where you come in. As it is, von Schonbeck may reach his objective and scoop the pool before we can get there.'

'But how are aircraft going to operate in the locality of these islands, with the nearest base more than two thousand miles away?' demanded Biggles.

'There will be a base nearer than that,' declared the Air Commodore. 'We are going to establish one.'

'Where?'

'Kerguelen Island. Five million pounds are at stake and that's a lot of money. The British supply-sloop, *Tern*, is already on its way to Kerguelen from the Falkland Islands, carrying food, stores, oil, petrol and other things you will be likely to require.'

'And we, presumably, shall take up residence on Kerguelen, and from there proceed to engage ourselves in a task compared with which the finding of a needle in a haystack becomes a simple matter?'

'That, exactly, is the idea,' agreed the Air Commodore.

'You'll pardon me for saying that it doesn't set me on fire with enthusiasm.'

'It should be interesting.'

'What should be interesting – the sea? Millions of miles of nothing but water? Water in large quantities always looks alike to me. There's a limit to the time I can look at it without getting bored.'

The Air Commodore smiled. 'When can you be ready to start?'

Biggles shrugged. 'Tomorrow, I suppose. That is, we can start ambling towards the Southern Hemisphere. I take it that we can make our own arrangements for getting to Kerguelen?'

'Of course.'

'When will the *Tern* be there?'

'She'll be there before you.'

'And having found the U-517, what do we do about it – always bearing in mind that if von Schonbeck spots a British aircraft prowling around he'll know why it is there – and not forgetting that his ship carries the latest thing in anti-aircraft guns?'

'You'll report its position by radio and endeavour to keep it in sight.'

'Why not sink the blighter and have done with it – if you see what I mean?' suggested Bertie.

The Air Commodore looked pained. 'By the time you find the U-517 it will probably have the gold on board. Five million pounds at the bottom of the Indian Ocean is no earthly use to anyone.'

'Of course – absolutely. Silly ass I am – what?' murmured Bertie apologetically.

'How many men comprise the crew of the U-517?' asked Biggles.

'Twenty-five, including the captain – all selected seamen.'

'Rather more than we could handle if we caught up with them somewhere.'

'Definitely. This crew fought the British Navy for three years – and got away with it. They must be tough. We'll get them if we can, but the gold must be our first consideration. Any more questions?' Biggles thought for a moment. 'I don't think so, sir. If anything occurs to me I'll let you know. Meanwhile, I'd better start making arrangements.'

'Good. The Navy is still on the job. If we get any signals I'll pass the information on to you. You get yourselves to Kerguelen for a start. The *Tern* will be there. The skipper has orders to reconnoitre for the best landing-area. He is letting us know the precise position. You'll have to use a marine aircraft, of course – presumably a flying-boat.'

'I don't feel inclined to try putting a land machine down in a bog,' murmured Biggles.

'Quite. With a flying-boat, from Kerguelen you'll be able to cover a pretty wide area. There's really no need for me to warn you, I know, but for heaven's sake be careful with your navigation. Sitting here, Kerguelen may sound a big mark to fly on, but there's an awful lot of water where you're going, and if you miss the island there'll be nothing between you and the South Pole.'

'I'll watch it,' promised Biggles, rising. 'Come on chaps – we'd better look out our winter woollies.'

CHAPTER III

Von Schonbeck Strikes First

'There is always a peculiar fascination in watching a ship put to sea, but on this occasion it means more than usual – a lot more.' Biggles spoke. With the others standing beside him he was watching the *Tern*, a speck in a world of restless water, standing away to the western horizon, with the wind, blowing half a gale, tearing the smoke from her funnel and beating it down into a backwash of flying spray.

A fortnight had elapsed since the conversation with Air Commodore Raymond at the Yard, a busy fortnight in which they had transported themselves from the centre of civilisation to the fringe of the known world. In that time there had been no word of von Schonbeck or the U-517. Not that this surprised Biggles. As he remarked, with the oceans of the world from which to choose, the cleverest U-boat commander in the Nazi service would not find it hard to disappear.

For the rest, the preliminary preparations had gone, to use a well-worn expression, according to plan. The captain of the *Tern*, a cheerful young lieutenant who had been invalided from the Fleet Air Arm, had done his job well, both in his selection of a site for the base and its establishment. At the end of a long, almost land-locked creek, protected on the windward side by a range of gaunt hills, had been erected two iron-roofed Nissen huts of service pattern. One was the mess, living-and sleeping-quarters. Packing-cases served for chairs and table. The most conspicuous article of furniture was a small but powerful radio instrument. The other hut housed the stores – tinned foods, spare parts, emergency repair kits and a few cases of small-arms ammunition. A short distance from these buildings was the 'dump', consisting of three circular erections of hand-picked stone, covered with tarpaulins, securely anchored against the wind. These contained petrol in the regulation four-gallon cans, oil, and a dozen depth-charges, aircraft type. A spring-fed burn, gushing noisily close at hand, provided unlimited water.

With the departure of the *Tern* the radio was the only link with the outside world, a world that now seemed as far removed as the moon. There would be no transmitting though, Biggles decided, except in case of emergency, for the obvious reason that signals might be picked up by the enemy, who was also equipped with wireless; but there was no reason why they should not listen to messages from home. Von Schonbeck, of course, would be able to hear these; but he would not know to whom they were directed, for the Yard call signal for the Kerguelen base consisted only of the cypher XL. Conversely, the party on the island would be able to pick up any messages sent out by von Schonbeck, although as far as they were aware there was no reason why the Nazi should use his wireless.

The last leg of the outward flight had been made in one hop from South Africa. Two aircraft were in commission, both of the same type to prevent duplication of spare

22

parts. They were twin-engined, flying-boat, amphibious monoplanes of the *Tarpon* class, war machines that had been specially designed for long-distance marine convoy work, and which were still on the secret list when the war ended. In the design of this aircraft, high speed, which is not essential for convoy work, had been sacrificed for robust construction and endurance-range, the two qualifications, declared Biggles, most to be desired for the task on hand. For reasons of weight limitation, armament had been arranged more for defence than attack – two fixed machine-guns mounted one on either side of the hull firing forward, and a similar mobile weapon covering the tail. The attack weapon of the *Tarpon*, against hostile marine craft, was the depth-charge, and the hull was equipped to carry two such charges of five hundred pounds each. In other respects, with the exception of some small arms, rifles and automatics which Biggles had added, the war-load was normal for a naval aircraft during the closing months of the war.

Biggles had flown out in one, with Ginger as second pilot. Algy and Bertie had flown the other. Biggles had resolved that in the ordinary way only one machine would be in the air at a time, the other remaining in reserve. He had no intention, he asserted, of marooning himself on a place like Kerguelen, without a means of getting off it. True, the Air Commodore knew where they were, and could always send out a ship or a relief aircraft; but it might be some time before the relief vessel arrived, and should a casualty occur the delay might mean the difference between life and death. Moreover, the only way help could be called was by radio, and should von Schonbeck pick up the SOS he might decide to come along and investigate – a contingency which, in view of the number of men at the German's command, Biggles preferred to avoid. Hence the two *Tarpon* aircraft.

The *Tern* had remained with them for two days. Then, after a final cheery meal on board, the robust little vessel had set off on the return passage to its station. Those who were to remain watched it forging its way, sometimes half-hidden by spray, across a desolation of water.

Ginger looked about him. The scene, both land and sea, was as melancholy a spectacle as could be imagined. It was a world without colour. The land, what could be seen of it, was mostly sheer rock – grim, black, basaltic cliffs. The sea was black, not the clear blue-black of ink, but a greenish black, except where tire wind caught it and whipped the surface to slaty-grey. The sky was like a dome of lead. A curtain of cloud, unbroken by a single rift, stretched from horizon to horizon. There was a feeling of rain in the air. Far to the south, an iceberg, draped in tenuous mist, was drifting sluggishly across the face of the water. A few gulls wheeled, screaming defiance at the intruders.

Ginger walked a little way to the crest of a hill that commanded a view inland. It was just the same. Not a tree broke the barren skyline. Not a roof. Nothing but rock and harsh, wiry grass pressed flat by the everlasting wind. The dominating impression conveyed by the picture was utter loneliness; not the friendly loneliness of a quiet spot in rural Britain, with telegraph poles on the horizon and the distant hum of traffic in the air, but a vast hostile loneliness that was like a cold hand on the heart, reminding a man what a puny thing he is compared with Nature untamed.

Ginger walked back – rather quickly – to the others. The *Tern* was hull down.

'Let's go inside and have another look at the map,' suggested Biggles.

They went in. Biggles unfolded his map on a packing-case and studied it for a little while without speaking. He had ringed the base in red ink. From it, radiating like the spokes of a wheel, were pencil lines to other islands. Beside each line was marked the distance and the compass course.

'I suppose the first place to explore is Kerguelen,' said Biggles, glancing up. 'From the air it shouldn't take long. If von Schonbeck's secret depot is somewhere here on the island we ought to see it. I can't believe that a number of men can use any place for three years without leaving traces visible from above, no matter how careful they may be. But there is one big snag against aerial reconnaissance. I own that I did not realise it until we got here and saw the sort of place we were in. If von Schonbeck is in fact established on Kerguelen, he'll see us – or our aircraft – before we see him.'

'What of it, old boy?' asked Bertie.

'Only this,' said Biggles slowly. 'Not being a fool, von Schonbeck will realise instantly why an aircraft is in this part of the world. He'll know that it doesn't take many men to maintain a machine. He may decide to play the same game as ourselves. That is, he may come gunning for us. He has twenty-five men. There are four of us. I don't object to numerical odds, within reason, but if the hare suddenly became the hunter we might find ourselves in a mess. We should have to bolt – and consider ourselves lucky if we got away. That would be a pretty state of affairs to report to Raymond, wouldn't it?'

'But we could call Raymond on the radio and tell him where von Schonbeck has his hide-out – if I make myself clear?' suggested Bertie. 'Raymond could send out a whole bally fleet of destroyers.'

'Yes, he could,' admitted Biggles, with bitter sarcasm. 'And by the time they got here von Schonbeck would be a thousand miles away with the gold under his conning tower.'

'By Jove! Yes. Never looked at it like that – silly ass I am,' muttered Bertie.

'If we can't fly to make our reconnaissance, what's the answer?' asked Algy.

'We shall have to fly, of course,' returned Biggles. 'But before we take off I think we ought to do a bit of foot-work, to make sure that the Nazis are not sitting on our doorstep. When we have made certain that they are not within striking distance, at any rate, we can start flying.'

'But if we spot the submarine depot it comes to the same thing,' asserted Ginger. 'How are four of us going to attack twenty-five?'

'We couldn't,' admitted Biggles. 'Our play would be to sink the sub, if it was in shallow water, or put it out of action. That would keep the Nazis here, as safe as if they were in prison, until the Navy could collect them.'

'This is all assuming that the Nazis are at their base,' put in Algy. 'What happens if we spot the U-517 at sea? We shall have no means of knowing whether or not it has the gold on board. If we sink the sub, bang goes the gold, and the whole object of the expedition will sink with it. If we don't sink the sub it will simply submerge when it sees us and get away. Then we have to start looking all over again.'

'I've considered all these snags,' averred Biggles. 'Frankly, I can't see how we can make a definite plan. The only thing we can do is wait until we do spot the submarine, and then act for the best as the conditions suggest. We're just as likely to spot the sub at sea as in some anchorage. No doubt it will travel on the surface for normal operations – I mean, until it hears us or sees us. Anyway, whether we like it or not, von Schonbeck will have to spend a certain amount of time on the surface to charge his batteries. During the war that was usually done at night. We may do some night flying – high-altitude work – while there is a moon. The best thing of all would be to find the submarine base while the U-boat is absent, perhaps before it gets here, and destroy the fuel supply. Von Schonbeck must be relying on finding oil at his secret base. Without it he would be helpless. He couldn't get anywhere. He'd just have to stay where he was, and that would suit us very nicely. The big question is, has von Schonbeck reached his base yet? We don't know and we've no means of finding out until we spot the sub, in which case its course should tell us something. Admiralty experts know pretty well the speed of the U-517 class of submarine, and they assured me before I left London that it couldn't get here to Kerguelen, if this was its objective, before the twenty-fourth. This is the twenty-first. If they are right we still have three days. They may be wrong. Von Schonbeck may have a card up his sleeve. Again, the sub may not be heading for Kerguelen. The gold may be on some island nearer to the mainland.'

'It all sounds pretty vague to me,' sighed Bertie.

'It is vague,' admitted Biggles. 'We shall just have to do the best we can with the data available. We're here, anyway, and that's a start. We've no time to lose. Once von Schonbeck gets to his hide-out it won't take him long to load up his gold and turn his nose towards South America. We must nab him before he starts on that tack or we shall need more than luck to catch him. If—'

Biggles broke off, tense, in a listening attitude, as from far away there came three unmistakable gunshot reports – a single shot closely followed by two more. He looked at the others, sprang to his feet and made for the door. Before he could reach it, the hut vibrated with the long dull roar of a distant heavy explosion.

Another moment and Biggles was outside the hut, gazing in the direction in which the *Tern* had last been seen. Twilight was darkening a world already gloomy, so at first nothing could be seen except the vast expanse of empty sea; but after a little while it became possible to discern a smudge of smoke being blown along the horizon by the wind. Without a word Biggles ran to the nearest aircraft, cast off and jumped aboard. The others followed. Biggles was busy for a moment in the cockpit. The engines came to life, to roar – as it seemed – defiance to wind and wave. The machine moved, swinging round in a swirl of foam to face the open sea. In two minutes it was in the air, heading for the smoke which was now dispersing.

'What was it, do you think?' asked Ginger, who was sitting next to Biggles.

'I don't know,' answered Biggles in a hard voice, 'but I've got an idea. I hope I'm wrong – but I'm afraid...'

He zoomed to a thousand feet and then put the aircraft back on an even keel. What he was thinking Ginger did not know – but he could guess. For his eyes, too, were on the smoke. There was nothing else. Whatever had been under it, to cause it, had gone. From their elevated position the *Tern* should be in view. But it was not. There was nothing beside the smoke – nothing except the grey, heaving ocean.

Reaching his objective Biggles banked slightly, continuing the bank into a circle, looking down through a side window with eyes that were never still. 'Look for a conning tower or a periscope,' he snapped. 'If you see anything start to break surface, yell.'

Ginger did not answer. He, too, was staring down. There was little to see – a spreading patch of oil, some debris and a raft on which two men were lying prone. They did not move. He moistened his lips, which had gone dry.

'I'm going down,' said Biggles, 'keep watching.' He subjected the area to a final searching scrutiny and then landed near the raft, taxi-ing on until one wing was over it. 'Take over,' he ordered curtly, and climbing out ran along the wing until he could drop on the raft.

Out of the corners of his eyes Ginger saw him take one look and clamber back. 'All right,' he said. 'I'll have her.' He dropped into his seat and took off, climbing steeply to resume his scrutiny of the ocean.

'How about those fellows? Are we going to leave them there?' asked Ginger.

'There's nothing we can do for them – they're dead,' returned Biggles shortly. 'I daren't hang about. We might get what they got.'

Algy came forward. 'What was it – the *Tern*?'

'Yes. With a hole blown in her side by a torpedo, she must have gone down like a broken bottle.'

'How do you know it was a torpedo?'

'It couldn't have been anything else. She didn't blow herself up and gunfire wouldn't have sent her down in five minutes. Two men got away on that raft. I remember them well – two nice lads, they were. Now they're dead. Riddled with bullets. There can't be many swine in the world who'd do a thing like that. Von Schonbeck is one of them. This is his hunting-ground. He's back at his old game.'

'Does that mean he knows we're here?' asked Algy.

'Not necessarily. At least, it's unlikely that he knew when he fired the torpedo, although he probably knows now.'

'Then why should he do a thing like that?'

'The *Tern* was a British ship. Spite would be ample motive for a Nazi of von Schonbeck's type.'

'What do you think happened?' asked Ginger.

'The skipper of the *Tern* knew all about the U-517,' answered Biggles. 'In fact, he told me that he'd been ordered to keep an eye open for her. I'd say the ship spotted the submarine, running on the surface, and fired a shot across her bows to halt her. Von Schonbeck answered with a torpedo. The *Tern* would see it coming and have time to fire two more shots before it hit her. One torpedo was enough. After that von Schonbeck followed his usual procedure of destroying evidence by machine-gunning the survivors.'

'To do that he must have stayed on the surface.'

'Of course. He dived when he heard us coming.'

'You think he heard us?'

'Bound to. Had we not come along he'd probably still be on the surface, gloating.'

'So he knows we're here?'

'He knows there's an aircraft in the vicinity. He may not know why, but from what we know of the man he must have a pretty good idea.' Biggles raised his eyes from the water. 'Well, it's no use looking for him now; he'll stay submerged until he's well out of the area.'

Biggles flew back to the base and landed. No one spoke while they were tying up. Ginger was depressed, appalled, by the tragic end of the *Tern* and its cheerful company. Grim-faced, Biggles strode on to the hut. He waited until the others were inside, with the door shut, before he spoke.

'This makes a difference,' he said, dropping on to one of the packing-cases that served as chairs. 'We've got to go back to war conditions. The first thing is a black-out – and when I say black-out I mean a real black-out. Von Schonbeck will have guessed by now that we are after him. At any rate, he must know that an aircraft is here; but he doesn't know where it is based, and I don t want him to know. No lights after dark, or he soon will know. The U-517 carries guns – heavy guns, too. If von Schonbeck located us he might well attack us. He could sit a mile away and shell us to blazes. But let's have supper and turn in. Tomorrow we'll give Kerguelen the once-over.'

'Von Schonbeck has a big advantage,' observed Ginger moodily. 'He can hear us when we're on the move, but we can't hear him.'

'Nevertheless he has a handicap that doesn't affect us,' asserted Biggles.

'What is it?'

'Oil. Oil is to a submarine what scent is to a fox – he can't move without it. The latest submarines are fitted with every conceivable device to prevent oil from escaping – special valves on the propeller shaft, and so on – but she still can't move without leaving a trace. It's impossible to keep the deck clear of oil. The guns need oil to keep them working smoothly. When a submarine dives some of that oil comes off, and in a smooth sea it only needs a few drops of oil to leave a stain, perhaps a trail. A sub that has been at sea for a long time, due to general wear and tear and perhaps a leaky plate or two, leaves a trail that can be seen for miles. The trouble during the war was, thousands of ships were on the move, all leaving trails. Damaged tankers were spilling hundreds of tons of oil. Planes were crashing in the sea, all spilling oil. But there's nothing here to spill oil – *except the craft we're looking for*. Okay. Fix a blanket over that window somebody and I'll light a candle.'

CHAPTER IV

Biggles Looks Around

After a fairly comfortable night, a night that passed without incident except that Ginger was more than once awakened by the howling of wildcats, break of dawn found Biggles outside the hut surveying the sea for signs of the U-517, and the sky for indications of probable weather conditions. The others joined him.

The prospect was not one to arouse enthusiasm. In the wan light of early dawn, land and sea looked even more depressing and bleak than on the previous evening. Ginger made a remark to this effect, whereupon Biggles replied, dryly, that as according to Admiralty Sailing Directions these conditions persisted for three hundred days of the year, the sooner they accustomed themselves to them the better. 'I was hoping to catch sight of the U-boat,' he added, 'but no doubt von Schonbeck is too wily a bird to surface near his latest sinking, knowing that an aircraft is in the offing. Still, we know he's arrived, and that's something. Moreover, he can't be far away. I don't mind telling you that the sinking of the *Tern* has made me sick and savage. It makes our account with this cold-blooded Nazi a personal one. Really, we ought to report the sinking to headquarters, but I don't feel inclined to risk giving our position away by using the radio. It will have to wait. Let's have breakfast and get busy.'

The meal over, Biggles picked up his binoculars. 'Before we start flying operations, as I suggested yesterday, I think we ought to have a look round from the nearest high ground to make sure that the U–517 isn't skulking in some hole within earshot. Algy, I shall have to ask you to stick around here and keep an ear to the radio in case any signals come through. I aim to be back by lunch-time, so see what you can turn out in the grub line.'

Biggles, Ginger and Bertie, set off, heading for a towering rock massif that rose up behind the camp at no great distance. During the climb, from time to time Biggles paused to scan the sea and coastline through his binoculars, but each time he returned the glasses to their case without comment. The summit was reached in just over an hour, and from there a long and careful reconnaissance was made of the view it commanded.

For some time nobody spoke, probably because there was no specific object to call for remark; but Ginger, as he surveyed the scene, was appalled by the fearful character of the place. It was worse, far worse, than anything he had imagined. To left and right ran a rugged coastline, sheer rock in most places rising straight out of the sea, sometimes to a height of not much less than a thousand feet. Into these cliffs, untold ages of corrosion had cut narrow inlets of depths varying from a hundred yards to a mile or more. Within these confines the water lay black and still. Here and there a mass of cliff had fallen, leaving numerous small islets to provide a perch for gulls, penguins and seals – the only living creatures in sight. Not a tree, nor even a bush of any size, could be seen. The only growth was a stiff wiry grass that bent under the breeze. This did not grow in broad patches, in the manner of turf; it occurred only in low-lying areas and sprang up in the form of great tussocks.

Biggles pointed to some that lay below them. 'I should be sorry to have to walk through that stuff. I'd wager it's peat bog between those tussocks. It looks like moss, and so it is, but if you stepped on it you'd probably go straight through up to the neck. I've seen that sort of stuff before, in northern Canada.'

Inland, the terrain rose in a succession of steps and screes to a considerable height before falling into what appeared to be a vast central basin, too distant for details to be observed.

'I say, old boy, what a place, you know, and all that,' remarked Bertie.

'As you say, it's a place,' agreed Biggles. 'Place is the word. The Nazi Higher Command knew what it was doing when it selected this God-forsaken area for a secret base. Not much risk of interference. Von Schonbeck has this advantage, and we should do well to remember it – having been cruising in these waters for three years he probably knows every hole and corner. We know nothing about it, and the chart shows very little, so if it comes to a matter of hide-and-seek he's likely to win the game. Take a look.' He passed the glasses to Bertie, who, after a while, handed them on to Ginger. Through them the stark inhospitality of the island could be fully appreciated.

'Before we go back we'll cut across to that shoulder of rock on the right,' decided Biggles. 'It blots out a lot of the sea that lies behind it. We may as well have a look at all there is to see while we're at it.'

'It all seems a pretty hopeless business to me, old lad, if you don't mind my saying so,' observed Bertie, as they descended. 'Instead of tearing up and down and round and round these bally rocks why not shoot across to the Magellan Straits and wait for the blighter to show up – nab him as he goes through – if you see what I mean?'

'It happens that the territory on either side of the Straits is not British, and there's no airfield, anyway,' answered Biggles.

'We could sit on the sea.'

'The sea would be more likely to sit on us,' asserted Biggles. 'From what I have heard of the Magellan Straits even the biggest ships reckon to take a pounding going through, in which case it makes no appeal to me as a parking-place for an aircraft.'

'Absolutely, old boy – absolutely,' agreed Bertie.

On the way to the new objective the party had to pass near the inner end of an inlet of some size. Here the rocks had tumbled down in a wild chaos of boulders to end in a short, rough shingle beach. Biggles stopped, looking at something. Putting up his glasses he looked again. Presently, without a word, he changed direction towards the object that had claimed his attention. Reaching it he said quietly, 'We needn't wonder what happened here.'

'Poor wretches,' breathed Bertie. 'Tough luck – what?'

Ginger did not speak. There was really nothing to say. What lay before them told its own story, and the story was one of shipwreck and disaster. A few rotting timbers that had once been a ship's life-boat lay just above the high-water mark. Strewn about were some empty biscuit tins and a water keg. More poignant than these was an oar that stood up with its lower part held in a cairn of stones; it had fallen askew, but from the blade still hung the tatters of what had once been a man's shirt. Nearby, under the lee of a rough windbreak of stones, lay five skeletons.

'God! What a place to be cast away,' breathed Biggles, in a voice low and vibrant with sympathy. 'What a hope they had. I wonder who they were? They managed to reach land, and this was the land they reached. A lot of good it did them.'

'Some of von Schonbeck's victims, who managed to get away,' suggested Ginger.

'Quite likely.' Biggles shrugged. 'Well, staring at these poor bones won't bring them back to life; we'll leave them here to their loneliness. They should help us to remember what happens to castaways on Kerguelen.' Striding on he led the way to the top of the rock that had been their goal. As he breasted the final rise he uttered an exclamation that brought the others quickly to his side. By that time the glasses were at his eyes, focused.

Following the direction Ginger made out a vessel about five miles way. 'A ship, by jingo!' he exclaimed.

'She looks like a whaler,' said Biggles, without lowering the glasses. 'It's unlikely that any other sort of ship would have business here.' He continued his scrutiny.

In fact, Ginger watched the ship for so long, with a deepening expression of surprise on his face, that he was constrained to ask, '*Is* it a whaler?'

'It is,' answered Biggles. 'Heading south-east.' He lowered the glasses a trifle.

'Now what can you see?' asked Ginger impatiently.

'I can see what looks to me suspiciously like a trail of oil. It starts out there in the general direction of the ship and runs back towards the southern tip of this island. That means she must have been here – or else she passed pretty close.'

'But the oil—'

'There's nothing remarkable about that,' broke in Biggles. 'A whaler, I imagine, would always leave an oil trail. Modern whalers render the blubber down on board, and I reckon a ship doing that would fairly drip oil, particularly if she had been through heavy weather. All the same…' Biggles shifted the glasses slightly and continued to stare. 'She certainly is losing some oil,' he went on. At last he lowered the glasses. 'I'd like to have a closer look at that ship,' he said slowly. 'After we've been home I think I'll fly out and give her the once-over. There's nothing else to be seen from here, so we may as well start back.'

As they approached the huts Algy could be seen standing outside, waiting.

'What's the news?' called Biggles.

'The air has been fairly buzzing with signals,' answered Algy.

'For us?'

'No – they're in code.'

'The deuce they are.' Biggles increased his pace until he came up with Algy. 'Were these two-way signals?'

'Yes.'

'Hm! That's interesting. We know the submarine is about. Von Schonbeck might use code. But who would he be talking to? What was the strength of these signals?'

'They sounded pretty close, to me.'

'Did you keep a record?'

Algy held out a sheet of paper.

Biggles glanced at it and shook his head. 'No use amateurs like us trying to decode that,' he muttered. 'Scotland Yard could do it, no doubt. They've specialists trained for the job. But to get this to the Yard and wait for a reply would be too slow to be any use.'

'Send the thing by radio,' suggested Bertie, polishing his eyeglass.

'And tell the people who sent out the signals that we've picked them up? Not on your life. If there are transmitters in the region you may be sure they'll have operators always on duty. Von Schonbeck will know where we are, soon enough. I'm keeping off the air until it's absolutely vital that we use it.'

'You think von Schonbeck was behind these signals?' suggested Algy.

'I don't think there's much doubt about it,' returned Biggles promptly. 'There's no need for anyone to use code now. Admittedly the Admiralty might use code, but it's unlikely that there are any warships within a thousand miles of us. The question is, who was von Schonbeck talking to? I wonder...' Biggles paused. 'From the top of the hill we spotted a whaler standing away to the south-east. As soon as I have gulped a spot of lunch I'm going to have a closer look at her.'

'But I say, old boy, there's no need for a whaler to use code,' protested Bertie.

'Not when her business is catching whales,' answered Biggles vaguely.

'Have you any reason to suppose that this one isn't catching whales?' queried Ginger shrewdly.

'I don't know,' answered Biggles thoughtfully.

'A whaler would be a very useful parent ship for a submarine – for refuelling, and so on. I had a good look at that ship this morning.'

'So I noticed,' put in Ginger.

'She was too far off for me to make out the flag she was flying, but there was something about her behaviour that struck me as odd.'

'What was it?'

Biggles took out a cigarette and tapped it on the back of his hand. 'It was this. A few miles to the east of that ship there was a school of whales. The look-out must have seen them. The business of a whaler is to kill whales, so one would have thought that the ship would have turned towards them. As far as I could make out it took not the slightest notice of them.'

'Perhaps it already had a full load?' suggested Algy.

'In that case why was it heading south-east, when it should have set a course for Europe or North America?'

'I see what you mean,' said Algy softly.

'We know the U-517 is in the vicinity – within, say, a couple of hundred miles at the very outside,' resumed Biggles. 'That being the case you may wonder why I haven't started a systematic combing of the ocean, looking for her. The answer is I want von Schonbeck to reassure himself that all is well. After he sank the *Tern* and heard us coming – if in fact he did hear us – he would dive, and stay submerged. It would be some hours before he surfaced. He would feel pretty safe last night, but with the coming of daylight he would certainly be on the alert. By giving him a rest we may catch him napping. In view of what we have seen today there seems a chance that the whaler is a German ship working with him. It may have a rendezvous with him. Let's have a look at the map to get an idea of where the whaler is making for. Speaking from memory there's nothing in that direction but water.'

Sitting on a packing-case Biggles opened the chart and looked at it. 'We needn't waste time on this,' he went on. 'If the whaler holds on the course it was making when we last saw her it will touch nothing till it comes to the polar ice-pack. The nearest land is here, this island to the east, although there's a doubt about that.' He pointed to a remote speck that carried the name Corbie Island (E.D.). 'Corbie Island, even if it exists, is two hundred miles away to the east of the whaler's last known position. It's a long way from here, but we'll have a look at it sometime. Meanwhile, let's eat. After lunch I'll take Ginger with me and have a look at these whale hunters. You, Algy, and Bertie, will stand by for radio signals, and be prepared to fly the spare machine if it is needed.'

The meal did not take long, for Biggles, when busy, occupied no more time with food than was necessary to support life. As soon as it was over he donned his flying-kit and strode down to the mooring. Ginger followed.

In a few minutes the aircraft was in the air, climbing towards the leaden cloudbank that still covered the sky.

CHAPTER V

The Whaler

At two thousand feet, just below the ceiling, Biggles levelled out and turned to the south-east. 'Keep your eyes mobile,' he said to Ginger. 'The U-boat may be about. Watch the creeks and inlets for oil tracks. The wind seems to be freshening again, so I'm afraid we shan't see much.'

Looking down Ginger regarded the surface of the globe, or as much as he could see of it, with morbid curiosity. Most of the island was now in view. The only part hidden was the southern tip where haze restricted visibility. As far as the land was concerned the spectacle offered nothing new; it was merely an extended version of what had been seen from ground level – an expanse of colourless wilderness, bleak and desolate in the extreme, with drab green areas marking the low-lying portions. These, he assumed, were the bogs referred to in the Admiralty description. The coastline was as irregular as the outside of an unfinished jigsaw puzzle. The sea offered even less to the eye. On every side it rolled away to pitiless distances, unbroken by any object except far to the south, where a line of icebergs and floes marked the outer defences of the polar regions. Of the submarine there was no sign, nor was the whaler in sight. The oil trail that Biggles had observed

43

was still there, a sinuous grey mark across the surface of the ocean, narrow at the head and widening towards the tail where it swung round in a mighty curve towards the southern tip of the island.

'I fancy the wind has veered,' remarked Biggles. 'That trail is not as clear as it was. If a sea gets up it will soon be wiped out altogether, but it's still clear enough to give us the general direction taken by the whaler. Hello! There are the whales, just breaking surface. The whaler doesn't appear to have interfered with them.'

Ginger gazed with curiosity at the sea-monsters, looking from the air rather like a line of torpedoes floating on the surface of the water. 'What are you going to do first?' he asked. 'Are you going to follow the oil trail to the ship or to the island?'

'For a start I'm going to have a close look at the ship,' answered Biggles. 'Then we'll come back and check up on where the oil starts from.'

'You said you'd expect a whaler to leak oil,' reminded Ginger.

'Yes, I know,' returned Biggles. 'But to leave a trail like that I reckon a ship would have to be losing more oil than seems reasonable. If it goes on, by the time she gets to port her tanks will be dry. Of course, it's always on the boards that she has been lying in the lee of the island refining blubber, in which case she would get pretty dirty. I'd like to spot the U-boat. She'll travel on the surface while she thinks she's safe.'

'With a snappy look-out on the watch for danger,' put in Ginger.

'No doubt.'

Ginger said no more. Biggles flew on, and soon afterwards his questing eyes picked up the whaler, hull down, over the starboard bow. 'There she is,' he said. 'Check up on her course.'

'I make it a point or two east of south-east,' declared Ginger a few minutes later.

'That's about it,' agreed Biggles. 'I wonder where she's making for – if she isn't hunting whales? Her present course won't take her to Corbie Island – at least, not if the island is anywhere near the position shown on the map. Of course, the island may not exist. The letters E.D. give us fair warning of that, so we can't blame the Admiralty if it isn't there.'

'This looking for an island that may not exist is an unsatisfactory business,' opined Ginger. 'I should have thought that by this time the Admiralty would have pinned down every square yard of dry ground between the Poles.'

'They'll do it now no doubt, now that we have aircraft with a range of thousands of miles,' answered Biggles. 'It would have been a long and tedious business to do it with surface-craft. There wasn't much point in it to justify the expense. No one wanted these islands, anyway. Air transportation has now given remote islands a new value, as refuelling stations for trans-ocean runs.' As he finished speaking Biggles cut the throttle and began to glide towards the whaler, now in full view some three or four miles distant. 'Hello! Did you notice that?' he asked sharply.

'She's changed course – if that's what you mean,' replied Ginger. 'You can tell that by the wake. She's heading pretty nearly due east now.'

'Quite right. She's only just spotted us. I wonder why she changed course? And come to think of it, that vessel must have been travelling flat out to cover as much water as she has since we last saw her. What was the reason for that?'

'Maybe she's a modern ship.'

'She must be, to travel at that rate.'

The aircraft dropped lower, rapidly overhauling the object of the conversation. Men could be seen on the deck, looking up. One waved. A flag fluttered to the peak.

'She's Norwegian!' cried Ginger.

'Say she's flying the Norwegian flag,' corrected Biggles. 'It isn't quite the same thing. A dishonest ship can fly any flag. Still, I believe Norway has the biggest whaling fleet afloat, so there would be nothing remarkable if she was Norwegian. Pity we can't make out her name, but we shan't be able to see it from the air.' He made a circle round the ship, which held on her course.

'Let's try being friendly,' suggested Biggles. He opened a side panel and waved.

The men on the deck of the ship, seven or eight of them, waved back.

'Can we speak to them?' asked Ginger.

'No,' answered Biggles. 'If we ask them who they are and what they are doing they might tell us anything, and we should have no means of checking up on it. If she is a consort of the U-boat we should merely reveal that we were suspicious of her without gaining anything.'

'Then there's nothing else we can do,' said Ginger.

'Nothing. We may as well go back. No use wasting petrol. We shan't learn anything more here.' Biggles turned away and started back over his course, keeping

46

parallel with the oil trail. 'I still say that ship is losing more oil that she should,' he murmured pensively.

He did not speak again until Kerguelen was almost under their keel. Then he said, 'There's the end of the oil trail, plain enough. The ship must have been lying in that cove.' He pointed. 'I think we'll go down and have a look round.'

Dropping lower, the aircraft passed over a narrow neck of water, not more than a hundred feet wide, with precipitous sides, and found herself over an almost circular cove of some size. As a harbour it was perfect, as perfect as anything an architect could design, yet from the sea its existence would not have been suspected.

'Spare my days!' exclaimed Biggles. 'Look at the oil! That whaler must have burst a tank to make all that mess. I don't like the look of it. Keep your eyes skinned for anybody or anything moving. This is just the sort of place von Schonbeck would choose for a hide-out.' He put the machine in a turn and held it so until they had made three complete circuits at a height of less than a hundred feet. 'Of course, this may be a bona-fide whaling depot,' he went on. 'It's a depot of some sort, there's no doubt of that, and the place has been used recently. That's a camp down there.'

'I don't see any camp,' said Ginger.

'Look again,' invited Biggles. 'Look beyond that strip of shingle beach at the inner extremity of the cove. Those lumps are too square and regular to be natural rock formations.'

'Ah,' breathed Ginger. 'I get you.'

'We'll go in,' decided Biggles. 'If you see a movement, yell. I've got a feeling we're on the track of something.'

47

For a moment or two Ginger could see no movement of any sort, and he said so; then he cried out tersely; 'Steady! What's that – between the rocks? There's something moving. It's a—'

He was cut off by a blinding flash followed a split second later by an explosion so violent that the blast, striking the under-surfaces of the aircraft, caused it to yaw wildly.

Biggles slammed on full throttle and zoomed. 'What the deuce?!'

Ginger looked about him in no small alarm, fully expecting to see the smoke of a shell-burst, for he thought, naturally, that they had been shot at. But the sky was clear. The only smoke was a grey cloud that drifted across the cove from the point where the explosion had occurred. He continued to watch. Biggles continued to fly around, taking evading action.

'What in thunder was it?' he questioned, wonderingly.

'I don't know,' replied Ginger, in an astonished voice. 'I was just going to say that the thing I saw moving was a pig.'

'A *pig*! Ah. It must have been one of the wild hogs. So what? Hogs don't handle guns.'

'It may not have been a gun,' suggested Ginger.

'I think you've got something there,' returned Biggles in a curious voice. 'Let's try again.' He throttled back and put the machine in a new glide towards the anchorage. Nothing happened. The only sound was the gentle sighing of wind over the planes. On the ground nothing moved. The machine went on down, Biggles flying with one hand on the stick and the other on the throttle ready for instant action. Still nothing happened, and presently the machine landed, to run to a standstill near the beach, a position from which signs of human occupation ashore were at once evident. The keel of the aircraft grated gently on the shingle, where several gulls with oil-smeared wings tried in vain to take flight. Some lay dead.

'This place has a suspicious smell about it,' said Biggles quietly. 'But the smell I can smell isn't whales. It's machine oil.' For a minute or two longer he sat still, eyes active, hand on the throttle ready for a quick move; but nothing happened, and presently, satisfied, he relaxed. 'Let's go ashore,' he suggested.

Ginger went forward, dropped the anchor and stepped down into two feet of oil-coated water. Biggles joined him, and together they walked slowly up the beach towards three small rock buildings that Biggles had observed from the air. Ginger was quickening his pace when Biggles laid a restraining hand on his arm. 'Just a minute,' he said in a tense voice. 'Take a look at that.' He pointed.

Ginger stared with startled eyes at the object towards which Biggles had directed a finger. At first he could not make out what it was, although it had a sinister look about it. It appeared to be a red stain, surrounded by red splashes. Some loose, soft-looking fragments lay on it. 'My gosh!' he exclaimed in a horrified voice. 'It's blood.'

'It couldn't be anything else,' said Biggles.

'What do you make of it?'

'I don't make anything of it – except that somebody, or something, has just met with a nasty accident. That blood's fresh.' Biggles spoke, but he did not move. The muscles of his face were tense. His eyes were never still for a moment;

they went from point to point, always returning to the gruesome stain.

Ginger's eyes, too, were taking in every detail of the scene. It was now obvious that the place was, or had been until recently, a camp. The main features were the three huts, or cabins. There were other, smaller erections. All were built of the rock of which the island was composed so that they blended into the background and could not have been seen from a distance. Faint tracks led from hut to hut, and to the beach. There were a few other objects, none conspicuous in itself but together giving the impression of human occupation – a heap of driftwood, an empty can, a scrap of paper, a piece of orange peel. There was one very curious object. On a flat boulder, about thirty yards from where they stood, rested a biscuit tin. The label it bore was new, untarnished by weather. Biggles looked at it for some time. Then he moved, slowly, step by step, towards the ugly stain and the fragments that lay on it. Stooping, he touched a piece.

Ginger was nearly sick when he realised suddenly what it was. His lips curled as he muttered, 'Flesh!'

Biggles laughed – a short nervous laugh. 'Call it meat,' he corrected. 'You said you saw a pig – a wild hog?'

'Yes.'

'This was it. Something tore it to pieces – small pieces. And I've got a pretty good idea what it was.'

'It could only have been a bomb.'

'Something of the sort. The poor beast took fright at our arrival, and was running away – stop! Where do you think you're going?' Biggles's voice was crisp.

Ginger had moved forward. 'I was going to see what was in that biscuit tin,' he explained.

'It might be better to find out without touching it,' suggested Biggles grimly. 'Lie down.'

'Lie—?'

'Don't argue. Lie flat.'

Ginger, his face a picture of astonishment, obeyed.

Biggles also lay down. He drew his pistol and took careful aim at the tin.

Ginger waited.

'Hold your hat,' said Biggles curtly. His pistol spat. The tin moved a few inches, that was all. He fired again. This time the track of the weapon was followed by a vicious tearing explosion and the shrill whine of flying splinters. Grey smoke drifted. Debris pattered down. Silence returned.

Staring, Ginger saw that the tin, and most of the rock on which it had rested, had disappeared. His voice, when he spoke, was thin and dry with shock. 'What the dickens was that?'

'Booby trap,' answered Biggles quietly. 'That wretched hog saved *our* bacon,' he added with grim humour. 'Nazis have been here. We shall have to watch where we are putting our feet. And I'll tell you something else. Nazis don't set booby traps for penguins or wild hogs. Von Schonbeck knows we're here.'

CHAPTER VI

Tragedy Ashore

Ginger, looking thoroughly shaken, rose slowly to his feet, glancing around with no small apprehension. 'I don't like this place,' he decided. 'Let's get out of here.'

'I don't like it either, but we shall have to look at it,' answered Biggles.

'You think this was von Schonbeck's camp?'

'Yes – either his main base or an emergency depot.'

'Why not wait for him to come back?'

'Unless I have missed my guess he isn't coming back. Had he been coming back he would have left a guard over the place, and he would hardly have set booby traps. No, this was von Schonbeck's dump; when he went he went for good.'

'With the gold?'

'I don't think so,' said Biggles thoughtfully. 'I look at it like this. Whether this was von Schonbeck's base or not he was pretty certain to have a refuelling station on Kerguelen, which, after all, is the biggest island in the South Indian Ocean. He probably arrived about the same time as the *Tern*, or soon afterwards. Naturally, he would wonder what she was doing here, and watch her. He may have guessed the truth. Anyway, I'm pretty certain he saw us arrive, or heard us take off when he sank the *Tern*. For whom, except us, would he have set booby traps? He realised that he couldn't very well use Kerguelen at the same time as an aircraft without being spotted, so he cleared out, and knowing that sooner or later we should spot this camp, made arrangements for our reception. The booby trap is a Nazi specialty. Had that hog not come nosing around we might have stepped right into the trap, too.'

'But how does the whaler fit into the picture? Her trail brought us here.'

Biggles considered the question. 'I don't know – yet. We may find out presently.'

'If this was one of von Schonbeck's refuelling stations, and he's pushed off, it means that he had to abandon his oil. Yet he'll need plenty to get him to the Magellan Straits.'

'We'll see about that,' declared Biggles. 'Judging by the mess I'd say von Schonbeck has taken most of his oil with him. We'll soon see if that's true by having a look round, but, by thunder, we've got to be careful how we do it.'

'You're telling me,' muttered Ginger.

'Stay where you are for a minute.'

Biggles made a long and intensive survey of the camp before he moved, and then gave it as his opinion that provided they had only booby traps to deal with they were reasonably safe, now that they were alive to the danger. With his pistol he fired off two more rather obvious traps. One was a large flat stone, in the manner of a doorstep, at the entrance of the nearest hut; the other, inside the building, was a case of chocolate so arranged that anyone lifting the lid would be blown to pieces. Biggles took no risks, choosing his path carefully without touching anything that could be avoided. Several times he fired at suspected traps that turned out to be harmless. Very little had been left behind. As he remarked to Ginger, if von Schonbeck knew that he was being sought by the British authorities, as it was now evident that he did, it was unlikely that he would leave any clue to his whereabouts. A careful inspection revealed only a few cases of sundry stores, some emergency tools and boxes of ammunition.

The big discovery was a concrete oil-tank that had been sunk into the rock about fifty yards from the camp. It was nearly empty. Biggles pointed to a dark, even line that ran completely round the wall, about four feet above the present level of oil. 'That tells a story,' he remarked. 'For a long time the oil must have stood at the upper level, where it made a mark. That, I fancy, was the period when the submarine returned to Germany after the war ended. Within the last day or two the oil was reduced to its present level. What happened was, von Schonbeck came back and refuelled. There's one thing wrong with that argument, though. No submarine could have the capacity for the amount of oil that has just been taken from this tank – not in one loading.'

'Perhaps it made two trips. I mean, it could have shifted some of the oil and come back for more.'

Biggles shook his head. 'No, that won't do. Had two loads been taken there would have been a delay between the two loadings, in which case the oil would have made a second mark – a slight mark perhaps – where it rested in the interval. When the oil was pumped from this tank it was taken at one go.'

'Von Schonbeck may have chucked the oil away to prevent us from using it?' suggested Ginger.

'Goodness knows there's plenty of oil on the water.'

'I can't accept that,' replied Biggles. 'A gallon of oil, on water, will cover an area of miles. It only forms a very thin film. We're talking about tons of oil. Where has it gone? There is only one reasonable answer to that. If von Schonbeck did not make two or three trips, and I don't think he did – I doubt if he'd have the time, anyway – someone must have helped him. In other words, another vessel besides the submarine has been here. There aren't many ships in these waters. In fact, there's only one that could have done it – our friendly Norwegian whaler. This is all confirmation of our suspicion that the whaler isn't what she pretends to be. I'm almost certain now that the whaler is acting as consort to the submarine.'

'But would a Norwegian ship do that?'

'Not willingly – we needn't doubt that. But don't forget that von Schonbeck is a Nazi. We know something of his methods. The whaler might have been pressed into his service. Just how we don't know, but in due course we shall find out. In the meantime I shall work on the assumption that the whaler is acting with the submarine, carrying reserve oil.'

'It may have been doing that all along,' said Ginger. 'When Germany grabbed Norway she grabbed her ships.'

'That may be so, but I have a feeling that this is something new,' averred Biggles. 'Had the whaler been working with von Schonbeck during the war, Muller, the chap who was shot in Berlin, would have mentioned it in his statement. There's no doubt that a tanker would be invaluable to von Schonbeck, taking into consideration his proposed long run to Chile. Well, now he's got one.'

'What are we going to do about it?' inquired Ginger. 'If what you say is right, it would hit von Schonbeck a crack if we sank the whaler, but I imagine it wouldn't do to sink a ship on the high seas flying the Norwegian flag.'

'True enough,' asserted Biggles. 'It's a bit hard to know what to do, and that's a fact. It's no use our following the whaler because we couldn't do that without being seen or heard. The whaler would warn the submarine by radio that we were about. The two ships would certainly not make contact. In fact, it's more likely that the whaler would push off and lay a false scent to take us off the trail. But I think this is going rather far, considering all the evidence we have is circumstantial. We have no actual proof that the whaler is in the racket, although the fact that she is at this moment heading for nowhere in particular is in itself suspicious. Still, suspicion isn't proof.'

'You think that the whaler has a rendezvous with the submarine?'

'That, of course, is the obvious answer. The signals Algy picked up were probably messages between the whaler and the submarine. The sub could hide from us by submerging, but the whaler must stay on the surface, and from the fact that we turned up this morning to have a look at her she must know we are suspicious. At the same time, von Schonbeck is no doubt astute enough to know that we wouldn't risk a row with Norway by interfering with a ship flying the Norwegian flag. If, subsequently, we could prove that the vessel had been pressed into von Schonbeck's service it would be a different matter, but even then Norway would probably take a dim view of it if we sank one of her ships without consulting her. To report the situation to Raymond, who would then have to deal with the matter through diplomatic channels, would be hopeless. It would take weeks.'

'You're making it all sound very difficult,' argued Ginger. 'What *can* we do?'

'Before doing anything else we shall have to go home for some more fuel,' asserted Biggles. 'Then we might have another look at the whaler to check its course. There's just a possibility that we might strike the whaler and the submarine together – although I suppose that's hoping for too much. An alternative would be to locate this place Corbie Island and see what goes on there – if anything.'

'We could always track the whaler by following the oil trail,' suggested Ginger.

Biggles glanced at the sky. 'I'm not so sure of that. The wind is freshening and a heavy sea would soon wash out the trail.' He thought for a moment, tapping a cigarette on the back of his hand. 'There is one encouraging point arising out of all this. I don't think von Schonbeck has got the gold yet. The whaler is heading roughly south-east, so if our deductions are correct the sub has gone in that direction since sinking the *Tern*. If von Schonbeck had the gold on board surely he would be on a course north-west for Chile, going at full speed to get clear of this area as quickly as possible. We'll have a final look round and make for home.'

Without speaking again Biggles made another examination of the camp without discovering anything of interest. Finally he climbed to the top of a low cliff that backed the shingle beach to see what lay beyond it. Ginger followed, and looking round saw on all sides the dismal desolation to which he was becoming accustomed. The shoreline beyond the cove was now visible. It was dead, empty, except at one place where a flock of sea-birds were wheeling and swooping with a good deal of noise. Biggles raised his binoculars and studied the spot. He did not speak.

'See anything?' asked Ginger.

'I'm not sure,' answered Biggles slowly. 'But there must be something there or the gulls wouldn't behave like that. Maybe they're squabbling over a dead sea-creature – a whale, perhaps. I can just make out something tumbling in the surf, but I can't see what it is. Let's go and have a look. It isn't far.' He put his glasses back in their case and set off towards the clamour.

The walk took about ten minutes. Most of the gulls retired to a distance when the men approached; others hung about, circling, uttering the mournful cries of their kind. A short and rather dangerous descent took Biggles and Ginger to the shore, and after a final clamber over the rocks they reached their objective. They stopped. Neither spoke.

Near the rocks, rising and falling in the restless surf, were the bodies of two men, a short distance apart. Not without difficulty Biggles got one ashore, and a glance at the face was enough to tell Ginger that the man had not been dead for long – a few days at most. The body, as was to be expected, was that of an ordinary seaman, a tall, fair-haired, well-built fellow in the early twenties, clad in the usual blue jersey and trousers. There was nothing to indicate who he was. But the second body was more fruitful of information. This time it was an older man, grey and grizzled, his clean-shaven face tanned by wind and sun. He wore a jacket, and faded rings of gold braid on the sleeves revealed that he had been an officer. But what held Ginger's gaze was a small round hole, blue at the edges, over the right eye.

'This fellow wasn't drowned – he was shot,' said Biggles in a hard voice, as he felt in the inner pocket of the jacket. He brought out a number of letters. The ink of the addresses had run from immersion in the sea, but the words were still legible. In each case the name and address was the same. Biggles read it aloud. 'Sven Honritzen, Maritime Hotel, Oslo.' He glanced up and met Ginger's eyes. 'Norwegian,' he said laconically. 'The thing begins to hook together. This poor chap must have been one of the original officers of the whaler. I say original because I doubt very much if the officers now on board are Norwegians. The other fellow was a rating on the same ship. So the whaler *was* Norwegian. Von Schonbeck has been at his dirty work again. It doesn't need much imagination to read the story. The whaler was here on legitimate business. Unfortunately for the skipper von Schonbeck saw it and decided the ship would be useful to him as a mobile base. He may have given the crew the chance to work for him, or he may not. Either way it would have come to the same thing in the end. We know how von Schonbeck disposes of evidence. These men were murdered in cold blood. There may have been others. Von Schonbeck has taken over the ship, with a crew of his own on board, no doubt. Of course, there may still be some of the original hands on board, working under pressure. A Nazi would think nothing of shooting anybody who refused to work for him.' Biggles stared moodily at the bodies, the corners of his mouth turned down in hard lines. 'My God! The score against this inhuman devil is mounting,' he burst out suddenly, as if his passion had burst through his natural restraint. 'We'll get him. We'll get, him if we have to follow him to the Arctic and back again to the Antarctic! I'm always cautious about judging other men, but this cold-blooded brute isn't fit to five.' He recovered his composure with an effort, and went on slowly. 'Well, I suppose it's no use sitting here looking at these poor fellows. There's one last thing we can do for them. Give me a hand.'

The bodies were carried above the high-water mark. A grave in the rocks was out of the question, but plenty of loose rock was available, and at the end of half an hour a tall cairn marked the last resting place of two sailors who had gone down to the sea in a ship never to return.

Biggles unstrapped his flying-cap and requested Ginger to do the same. Then, with the salt wind ruffling his hair, and the gulls mewing a melancholy requiem, he said *The Lord's Prayer*.

'Amen,' said Ginger at the conclusion, and replaced his cap.

'All right,' said Biggles quietly. 'Let's go.' He set off at a fast pace up the cliff.

'Take it easy – what's the hurry?' complained Ginger.

'I'm anxious to have a word with von Schonbeck,' answered Biggles curtly.

Ginger glanced at his face and said no more. He had learned when not to talk.

CHAPTER VII

Ditched

Biggles hardly spoke on the way to the base, where the others were found waiting with some anxiety. They had no news, however, beyond a report of more signals so strong on the air that the transmitter was obviously at no great distance. But as these, as before, were in code, they conveyed no information beyond the fact that they had been sent.

Over lunch, for the benefit of Algy and Bertie, Biggles narrated the events of the morning. 'The most important thing about these developments is this,' he concluded. 'I'm pretty certain von Schonbeck hasn't picked up the gold yet or both he and the whaler would close down on radio signals and hit the breeze at top speed for South America. They'll get clear of this area as soon as they can, you may be sure; and that being so I feel inclined to prang the U-boat on sight – if we can find her. We could look for the gold afterwards. I'm not concerned overmuch with the whaler. It's von Schonbeck I'm after. The first thing to find is the U-boat.'

'Even if we located her I fancy we should have a job to catch her on the surface,' opined Algy. 'Von Schonbeck must know all there is to know about dodging aircraft.'

'I quite agree,' returned Biggles. 'But that submarine can't stay at sea indefinitely. She's bound to make a landfall somewhere, even if it's only to pick up the bullion. Our best chance is to catch her at moorings, and I'm going to have a shot at doing that this afternoon.'

'Where?'

'Corbie Island. In view of what we've seen that seems to offer the best chance. Even if the U-boat isn't actually there we might learn something.'

'Such as?'

'If the place has been used at all. If von Schonbeck is in the habit of using the island there are certain to be traces of his visits. If the gold is there he is bound to go there eventually, in which case he might find us waiting for him.'

'You've picked on Corbie Island on account of the course taken by the whaler, I suppose?' put in Bertie, polishing his eyeglass.

'Yes.'

'But the whaler wasn't actually heading for Corbie Island,' reminded Ginger.

'I wouldn't be too sure of that,' argued Biggles. 'Don't forget there is some doubt – a big doubt, in fact – as to the position of the island. You can bet your sweet life that if anyone knows just where it is it will be von Schonbeck. From a high altitude we ought to be able to spot it, even if it means quartering several hundred miles of water. I'm going to look for it, anyway. I'll take Ginger along – and a couple of depth-charges, in case they're needed.'

Bertie looked disappointed. 'I say, old boy, isn't it time we had a cut in?'

'Perhaps it is,' agreed Biggles. 'But for the moment I'd sooner play safe. In these waters you never know what you're going to run into, and I should feel a lot happier knowing that we had a machine in reserve. You and Algy stand by for a signal. If we need help I'll call you out. You'll get a turn presently.'

'As you say, old warrior,' sighed Bertie. 'You know best.'

Biggles finished his coffee and got up. 'Okay. Let's refuel and get off.'

Twenty minutes later, with Ginger at his side and two depth-charges on board, Biggles took off, and climbing steeply for height, headed for the estimated position of Corbie Island. Looking down Ginger observed from the 'white horses' that now flecked the sea that the wind had freshened to half a gale. For a short distance from the southern tip of the island a flat area marked the oil trail but, as Biggles had predicted, it was fading quickly in the more turbulent water.

For an hour Biggles flew on, his eyes for ever roving the forbidding waste of water. Icebergs came into sight far away on the starboard bow, and soon afterwards, the whaler.

'Take a look at her,' invited Biggles. 'She's back on her old course – that is, the course she was on when we first spotted her, before our arrival caused her to change it.'

'Are you going over to her?' asked Ginger.

'No,' decided Biggles. 'She wouldn't tell us anything if we did. We shall do better by keeping clear. The horizon is getting too hazy for my liking. Maybe it's only local; cold air in the region of the icebergs might cause that. If the wind veers to the north, bringing in warm air, it will probably get worse. We may have a look at the ship on the way back, but first of all I want to locate Corbie Island and plot its exact position.'

An hour later the aircraft was over the spot where Corbie Island should have been, according to the chart. It was not there. No land of any sort, not even a lonely rock, broke the endless procession of waves. Biggles re-checked his calculations and found them correct.

'Well, that's that,' he remarked. 'We can't blame the Admiralty. They gave us fair warning with the letters E.D. This is where we begin looking.'

'In which direction are you going to start?' inquired Ginger.

'The direction that the whaler was taking before she altered course,' returned Biggles. 'When she turned she was heading for the South Pole. Her skipper must take us for complete fools if he thinks we are to be kidded that he has business *there*. I'm more convinced than ever that the ship is making her way to Corbie Island. There's no other landfall she can make. And if the whaler *is* heading for Corbie Island she is being guided by von Schonbeck, or his men, not by the Admiralty chart.'

Biggles swung away on his new course. For twenty minutes he did not speak. Then a grunt of satisfaction left his lips. 'There it is,' he muttered. 'That's the island. So it *does* exist. It's only about eighty miles from the estimated position, and that isn't such a big margin of error considering the expanse of water involved. If we achieve nothing else we shall at least be able to correct the Admiralty chart,' he concluded dryly.

The aircraft flew on towards the island, now revealed as a strip of land some ten miles long by two or three miles wide, as rugged, barren and windswept as Kerguelen. Biggles made no attempt to conceal from possible watchers his intention of surveying the island, knowing such a course to be futile; for even if he took cover in the cloud layer overhead the engines would be heard – must already have been heard – by anyone on the island. So he throttled back and began a long glide towards his objective, with the result that by the time it was reached the aircraft was down to a thousand feet.

'By gosh! There's the sub!' cried Ginger suddenly. 'She's there! We've got her!'

Biggles said nothing. The need did not arise, for he could see clearly the object that had provoked Ginger's exclamations. It was the submarine – or *a* submarine – and there could only be one underwater-craft at such a place. It was lying hard against a natural rock-quay, well sheltered from the weather in a snug little cove with an entrance wide enough to permit the passage of a fair-sized vessel.

Ginger kept his eyes on the mark. 'I don't see anyone moving,' he observed.

'If the sub is there you can bet the crew isn't far away,' returned Biggles grimly.

'What are you going to do?'

'I'm going to give von Schonbeck something that should keep him on that lump of rock until the Admiralty can send a destroyer along to pick him up,' answered Biggles. As he spoke his left hand moved towards the bomb release. With the other he straightened the aircraft until it was gliding on a direct course for the U-boat.

'Look out!' shouted Ginger suddenly, in a voice shrill with alarm, as nearly a score of men dashed out from places in which they had evidently been hiding.

Biggles did not answer. He flicked the throttle wide open and held on his course. The engines roared and the machine gathered speed.

An instant later the flak came up. And it came in such quantity and with such accuracy that Ginger was startled and amazed.

'Those fellows have had plenty of practice,' said Biggles through his teeth. His expression did not change nor did his eyes leave the mark.

Ginger held his breath. The aircraft still had a quarter of a mile to go and it was rocking through a hail of tracer shells and machine-gun bullets. It was hit, not once but several times. Ginger could hear metal ripping through wood and fabric. It seemed like suicide to go on, but he knew it was no use saying anything; he knew that nothing would cause Biggles to abandon his attack while he still had a wing to keep the machine airborne. He felt the machine bounce slightly as the depth-charges left their racks, and was shifting his position to watch their downward track when an explosion nearly turned the machine on its back. It plunged wildly as it recovered, but even so he thought they were down. Then, with fabric streaming from the port wing, Biggles was taking evading action, and taking it desperately.

'Did I get her?' he snapped, the object of the attack still paramount in his mind.

Ginger looked down but could see nothing clearly for smoke. He noted, however, that the smoke came from the position where the submarine had been. 'I don't know,' he told Biggles. 'If you didn't hit her it was a pretty close miss.'

Still pursued by fire the aircraft was down to a hundred feet, racing over the sea with the island slipping away astern.

'There's nothing more we can do here. I'm going flat out for home,' declared Biggles tersely.

'I shan't burst into tears over that,' answered Ginger. 'One run through that stuff was enough.' Biggles swung round on the homeward course. 'You'd better have a look at things,' he ordered. 'I'm afraid we were hit pretty hard.'

'I can smell petrol,' replied Ginger.

Proceeding with his inspection he saw that the aircraft had suffered considerably. There were several holes in the hull. Splinters of wood and broken glass lay about. Both wings were lacerated. A whole section had been torn out of the port wing where it had received the direct hit that had turned the machine over. These things did not worry him unduly, for the modern military aircraft is built to withstand punishment. The main thing was, the engines were still running, and while they continued to do so the machine would probably remain airborne. What did worry him though was the smell of petrol. Petrol was in fact slopping about the floor. Making his way to the main tank, two clouds of suffocating spray told their own story. He went back to Biggles.

'We've got it in the main tank,' he reported. 'Two holes – bad ones.'

'Can you plug them?'

'I doubt it, but I'll try.'

'Don't overdo it. If you feel the fumes are getting you down come back to me. We'll land and do the job afloat.'

'You'll never get down on that sea – it's running a gale,' declared Ginger. 'The hull is holed, anyway.'

'Do what you can.'

Ginger retired to the tank, and with the equipment provided for the purpose succeeded in plugging one of the holes. The second one was beyond him, but he did the best he could with it. When he had finished the inside pressure was still forcing petrol through the leak. Gasping for breath, for the fumes in the cabin were suffocating, he staggered back to Biggles and reported the situation.

Biggles glanced at the petrol gauge on the instrument panel. 'We shan't get home,' he answered calmly. 'Call Algy on the radio and ask him to come out to meet us. Tell him to stand by to pick us up when we hit the drink.'

'Do, you think we shall last as long as that – I mean, till he gets here?' asked Ginger anxiously.

'Frankly, no,' returned Biggles evenly. He altered course slightly.

'What are you doing?' queried Ginger.

'Making for those icebergs. There should be slack water under the lee of them. We shall stand a better chance there than on the open sea. Tell Algy what we're doing. Give him the position of the island, too. Tell him the sub is there, and my orders are that he carries on if he fails to find us in twelve hours.'

'Von Schonbeck will pick up the signal,' warned Ginger.

'We can't prevent it,' said Biggles. 'Get busy. We haven't much time.'

'Okay.'

Ginger went off to the radio compartment. One glance was enough. The instrument was a shell-shattered wreck, damaged beyond all hope of repair. He went back to Biggles, relieved that the aircraft was still running fairly smoothly. 'No use,' he reported tersely. 'The transmitter looks like a cat's breakfast.'

Biggles's jaws clamped a little tighter. 'I doubt if it would have helped us much even if it had been in order.'

'How – why?' asked Ginger sharply, not liking the expression on Biggles's face.

'Take a look outside.'

Ginger looked out through a smashed side window, and understood. Grey mist was closing in all round. There was no horizon.

'The wind's swinging round to the north,' said Biggles quietly. 'I was afraid of it. It's been inclined that way all day. The fog's getting worse, and it's getting worse fast. We should just have time to reach the 'bergs.'

'That'll be a lot of use if we're blanketed in murk,' said Ginger bitterly. 'Algy won't be able to find us even if he comes looking when we don't turn up.'

'Sitting on a 'berg won't be as bad as rocking on the open water trying to keep the sea out,' asserted Biggles. 'There's the ice, straight ahead. We should just about reach it.'

Biggles's prophecy was not far out. By the time the outlying 'bergs were reached the engines were choking as the fuel petered out, and the mist had thickened to a white clammy fog. There was fairly smooth water in the lee of a big 'berg, and towards this Biggles turned the aircraft. It did not take long to go down, for the machine had been forced to under a hundred feet to keep the sea in sight.

'I'm going down on that slack water,' announced Biggles. 'We'll see how she goes when we get her down.

If she fills with water faster than we can bale it out, or plug the holes, I shall try to run ashore on that floe at the tail of the big 'berg. I've enough petrol in the gravity tank to do that.'

'Get as close as you can,' implored Ginger. 'That water looks cold.'

'I daren't land too close for fear of tearing our keel open on submerged ice,' answered Biggles. 'I'll do the best I can, but I'm afraid we're going to get our feet wet.'

He landed about a hundred yards from the big 'berg. It was an anxious moment, but nothing happened except that the water started pouring through the holes instantly, as was to be expected.

'We're filling,' warned Ginger, who was watching. 'She'll be awash in five minutes if you stop.'

Biggles did not answer. He switched over to gravity, and under this new brief lease of life the engines carried the aircraft on and up a shelving bank of ice. There was a nasty crunching sound as the keel grated. In a few yards the friction brought the aircraft to a halt; and there it remained, half ashore, the tail trailing in the water, rocking gently in the swell.

Ginger crawled out on to the ice and tried to haul the machine higher but in this he was unsuccessful.

Biggles joined him. 'We have at least got our feet on something solid,' he observed optimistically. 'I think the machine will ride all right where she is unless a big sea washes her off, or' – he turned his eyes to where the high end of the 'berg towered above them – 'or unless that pile falls down on us.'

'Is it likely to?' asked Ginger; consternation in his voice.

'Quite likely. Lumps of ice break off a 'berg as she melts. A blink of sunshine melting one side can cause a 'berg to overbalance and turn turtle.'

'Then I hope the sun stays where it is,' said Ginger fervently. 'Don't tell me any more horrors.' He stared at the white pall that now hemmed them in. 'Curse the fog,' he muttered.

'Unfortunately cursing it won't shift it,' returned Biggles evenly. 'There is this about it. The thing cuts two ways. If Algy can't find us, neither will the whaler. Of course, there's a snag, and it's a nasty one – or it will be if the fog persists. We're drifting, and even when Algy realises that we must be ditched he will have no means of checking our drift. Consequently, if the fog lasts for any length of time we shall be miles off a straight course to the island. He won't know where to look for us. I hope we don't drift too far north.'

'Why north, particularly?'

'Because north is the direction of the temperate zone. The farther north we drift the faster will the ice melt. But let's have a look at the machine to see if there is anything we can do. It'll be something if we can put her in a condition to keep afloat – in case the ice starts melting under our feet.'

Ginger stared into the fog, blowing on his hands, for the air was bitterly cold. The breeze seemed to be dying. The only sound in the frozen world in which they stood was the crash and crunch of ice as distant 'bergs collided. He shivered.

'Come on,' said Biggles shortly. 'Let's get busy.'

CHAPTER VIII

Algy Takes a Hand

As the afternoon gave place slowly to a long dreary twilight, for the twentieth time – or it may have been the thirtieth – Algy left the hut, made an anxious reconnaissance of the sky and returned to Bertie, who was sitting by the radio.

Bertie raised his eyebrows.

'Not a sign,' informed Algy.

'Really?' Bertie looked puzzled. 'But I say, old boy, what on earth can they be doing?'

Algy shrugged. 'Ask me something easier. But I can tell you this. There's a change in the weather. It's getting colder. I'll tell you something else. If Biggles isn't back in half an hour we shall know he won't be coming back. He'll be out of petrol. That is, if he's been in the air all this time. Of course, there's a chance that he may have landed somewhere – Corbie Island, or maybe on Kerguelen.'

'What I don't understand is, why he hasn't made a signal – being as how he's so late – if you see what I mean?' murmured Bertie. 'He must know how anxious we are, and all that. This bally instrument is dead. Not a squeak.'

'So you said before,' answered Algy. 'That's what I don't like about it. Everything seems to have gone off the air. That may be coincidence, or it may not.'

'You think maybe there's something cooking?'

'Maybe. No use guessing. We can only wait.'

'How about going off in the spare machine to see if we can't spot anything?'

'Not yet,' decided Algy. 'You know what a stickler Biggles is for orders. He said stay here. If he came back in a hurry and found we'd beetled off on our own account he'd have a few short sharp words to say about it. We'll give him a bit longer.' Algy looked at his watch. 'If he isn't back in, say, half an hour, we'll go and have a dekko. I can't help thinking that if he was in trouble, ditched, for example, he'd get in touch with us. In fact, one would think that would be the first thing he'd do. We'll give him a bit longer.' Algy sat on a packing-case and stared at the floor.

Half an hour passed. The radio remained dead. The only sound that came from outside was the distant lap of water and the melancholy cries of sea fowl. Algy dropped his cigarette, put his heel on it and got up. 'Okay,' he announced. 'Something's wrong. Let's go and have a look round.'

Picking up his flying-cap he walked to the door, opened it, but instead of passing on he pulled up short on the threshold with an exclamation of dismay.

'What's wrong old boy?' asked Bertie quickly.

'Fog,' answered Algy. 'Fog, of all things. We're grounded.'

Bertie walked to the door and stared at a blanket of grey mist that was slowly blotting out the scene. He did not speak.

'That settles any argument,' said Algy wearily. 'Biggles must have seen this coming. If he could have got home he'd have come home. He's down, somewhere – and there's nothing we can do about it.'

'We can keep an ear open for him – put out flares and that sort of thing, if he should turn up,' suggested Bertie.

'We can listen, but I don't think we shall hear much,' retorted Algy dubiously.

His pessimism was justified. As darkness deepened the fog closed in, enfolding everything in its clammy embrace.

'We may as well go inside and make ourselves comfortable as stand out here in this perishing pea soup,' said Algy at last.

They went in and closed the door. Bertie lighted a lamp and for a while they discussed the situation that had arisen. But at the finish, as Algy remarked, there was still nothing they could do about it. 'While this fog lasts we're tied to the carpet,' he averred.

'If it lifts at daylight we'll have a look round. Meanwhile, we may as well get some sleep.'

Dawn, to his unspeakable relief, found the fog lifting, or dispersing. 'By thunder! It's cold,' he exclaimed. 'There must be ice about. Let's grab some coffee and get away.'

Ten minutes later the reserve machine was in the air with Algy at the controls, heading in the general direction of Corbie Island, the last known objective of the missing aircraft. The flight that followed was similar to that made by Biggles the previous day. Visibility was still far from good; indeed, after going some distance, right across their course a heavy bank of fog still clung to the sea.

'Better go over that stuff,' advised Bertie.

'No,' argued Algy. 'I'm staying low, where I can see the drink. Biggles may be on the water and I'm not going to risk passing him.' Taking the machine down to a hundred feet he put the nose of the aircraft into the fog, and a minute later received such a shock as he had seldom experienced. His eyes were on the water, just discernible through the mist. Something – he knew not what, unless it was a highly developed instinct for danger – made him look up and glance ahead. A white mass of what at first he took to be opaque mist towered above him. For a second the curious irregularity of its outline puzzled him; then, suddenly, he realised that what he saw was not mist, but solid ice. Snatching in his breath from sheer shock he dragged the control column hard over into his thigh, and as the aircraft swung back over its course, zoomed high. A gasp of relief left his lips as the machine merged into clear air.

'Here, I say, old boy, what are you playing at?' protested Bertie, who had been staring down at the water and so had not seen the 'berg.

'That fog has too many solid patches in it for my liking,' muttered Algy grimly, moistening his lips. 'We nearly rammed a thousand tons of ice. I ought to be kicked from here to Halifax for not having the sense to realise what was causing that murk. I'll take your advice and go over the top.'

'Absolutely – I should jolly well think so,' murmured Bertie. 'No joke ramming a beastly iceberg.'

The aircraft roared on.

Clearing the fog-belt Algy saw an open sea ahead. He scanned it quickly and anxiously, but of the missing aircraft there was no sign. 'I'm going right on to Corbie Island,' he told Bertie.

'Suits me, old lad,' replied Bertie.

They were nearly an hour finding it, for, like Biggles, they quickly ascertained that it was not at the position shown on the chart. Circling, and climbing at the same time, it was Bertie who saw the remote speck of land creep up over the horizon.

'Yes, that must be it,' agreed Algy, when Bertie called attention to it. 'We'll go and give it the onceover. If Biggles isn't there then I shan't know where to look, and that's a fact.'

A reconnaissance of the island revealed nothing – that is, no mark of occupation.

'There's a jolly little cove down there, suit a submarine very nicely I should think,' remarked Bertie as they circled.

'I see it,' returned Algy. 'I don't see anything in it though. In fact, I don't see anything here to detain us. We might as well get back.' He turned the nose of the machine on the homeward track.

The only thing that happened during the first part of the return trip was that the weather definitely improved. Indeed, a streak of pale turquoise-blue sky appeared behind a rift in a cloudbank. In view of this Algy was not surprised to note that the fog-belt had dispersed, leaving the drifting floes and 'bergs in plain view. Not that these meant anything to him. There was no reason why they should. As masses of ice they were merely things to be avoided – or so he thought until a shout from Bertie brought his eyes round, questioningly.

'Look! Over there!' cried Bertie, shaken for once from his inconsequential manner.

Following the direction indicated Algy saw what appeared to be an extensive black scar on a floe that formed the tail of an iceberg of considerable size. For a little while, as he flew nearer, losing height, he reserved his opinion. But when, with a sinking sensation in the stomach, he observed the charred and blackened remains of an aircraft, he knew the worst. Or he thought he did.

'That's them,' he said in a voice that he did not recognise as his own. 'They must have done what I nearly did – tried charging through the fog and hit the 'berg. They were burnt out. We'll go down.'

Bertie did not answer.

Algy went down to make a safe landing as near to the wreck as he dare, afterwards taxi-ing on to the edge of the floe. Having made the aircraft fast they went on together.

There was no doubt in Algy's mind as to what they would find. With the wreck he was not concerned. His eyes probed it, looking for two bodies, for experience told him that those in the machine could not have escaped. But he could see nothing that looked remotely like a body, and when at length he stood right against the burnt-out wreck, and could still see no bodies, he uttered an exclamation of amazement in which there was a suspicion of rising hope.

'They're not here,' he said in an incredulous voice.

'But I say, that's odd – deuced odd,' declared Bertie, polishing his monocle furiously.

'I don't get it,' asserted Algy, looking around. 'Hello! What's this?' he went on sharply, and moved swiftly towards a stain on the ice some twenty paces from the wreck. It was red. There was one small splash with a few odd drops around it.

'I say, old boy, that's blood,' said Bertie, stooping. 'One of them must have been hurt.'

'That's obvious,' returned Algy. 'All the same there's something queer about this. If one of them was hurt badly enough to make a mark like this surely there ought to be a trail of blood leading from the machine to this point.'

'One of them might have been pitched out when the machine struck the ice,' suggested Bertie.

'It's just possible, but in that case I should have thought the mark in the ice would have been more definite,' returned Algy. He examined the ice critically. 'Yet I don't know,' he went on pensively. 'There are faint signs, marks, that a body could have made, lying here. But where are they now? With the machine burnt out they had no means of getting off this 'berg.' He turned bewildered eyes to survey the seascape. Nothing moved anywhere, only icebergs, icebergs with dark blue water between them. A feeble sun glinted on the tips of the big 'bergs. 'I don't know how it was possible, but the indications are that the injury that produced the blood was caused after the machine landed,' concluded Algy.

'Here, I say, what about this for an idea?' went on Bertie. He pointed to a tall pinnacle of ice that rose above the floe on which they stood. 'Now then. If a plane collided with the top of that 'berg it would be bashed about no end. Lumps of ice would be knocked off and fall to the bottom. I don't see any broken ice. And by Jove! I'll tell you something else. If a plane collided with solid ice the longerons would be buckled like corkscrews – wouldn't they?'

'Yes,' conceded Algy.

Bertie pointed to the remains of the machine. 'The longerons are as straight as crankshafts,' he declared.

'True enough,' agreed Algy. 'What you mean to say is, the machine didn't crash?'

'Absolutely.'

'But if it didn't crash why should they land here?'

Bertie shook his head. 'Ah! Sorry, old boy, but I don't know the answer to that one.'

'Okay. Then let's say that for some reason unknown Biggles landed here voluntarily,' resumed Algy impatiently. 'So what? Neither Biggles nor Ginger would be likely to set fire to the machine.'

'No, they would not,' agreed Bertie.

'Then who did?'

'You tell me,' pleaded Bertie. 'I'm no bally detective.'

Suddenly Algy took a pace forward and for a moment stood staring at something that projected from the blackened engine cowling; then he wrenched it out and held it up for Bertie's inspection. 'Look at that!' he exclaimed in an understanding voice. 'That isn't part of an aircraft. That's a piece of shell casing. Flak, by thunder! That's the answer. Now we're getting somewhere. Biggles found the submarine. He bombed it and got shot up. Remember the two depth-charges he carried? They're not here. Why not? Because he used them. Fool that I am for not spotting that immediately. The machine was hit, forced down and landed here. That's it. That's what happened.'

'And what happened next?' queried Bertie.

'The machine took fire on landing and was burnt out. One of them must have been wounded but didn't start to bleed until he was clear of the machine.'

Bertie nodded slowly. 'All right. One was wounded. He lay on the ice, bleeding. The other stood by. Then I suppose they both jumped into the sea?'

'Don't be a fool,' snapped Algy.

'Then what happened to them?'

Algy walked back to the bloodstain, stared at it for a little while, and then started casting around in increasing circles. He stopped suddenly and let out a yell. 'Here we are!' he cried. 'This is the way they went.'

Bertie joined him and saw at his feet odd spots of blood forming an irregular trail. Following it, he quickened his pace when he saw a small object lying on the ice some distance ahead. Reaching it, he picked it up. It appeared to be a small piece of bloodstained rag.

'That's Biggles's handkerchief,' said Algy in a dull voice.

They continued to follow the trail, with the drops of blood occurring farther and farther apart. It ended where the ice ended at the sea.

Automatically Algy raised his eyes and followed the trail out to sea as if it continued there. He started and clutched Bertie's arm. 'My God! Look there!' he cried in a strangled voice.

Bertie looked. A quarter of a mile away two polar bears were swimming strongly towards another 'berg.

For a little while time stood still. Without speaking, Algy and Bertie watched the bears reach their objective, clamber on the ice and then turn to stare at them. One uttered a hoarse growl. Its breath showed white, like smoke.

'I don't think it's much use looking for bodies here,' said Algy.

'Nor I,' returned Bertie.

They turned away.

CHAPTER IX

What Happened on the Ice

Algy's summing up of what had occurred on the iceberg was correct to a point.

Following their discussion on the situation Biggles had made a systematic inspection of the machine in the hope that it might be made serviceable as a surface-craft, if not as an aircraft. 'What I should really like to know is, did I hit that submarine?' he remarked as he worked.

'If you didn't actually hit it you were pretty close,' Ginger assured him.

'I don't know much about submarines, but I imagine that any sort of serious damage would keep the U-boat where she is for some time,' went on Biggles. 'Quite aside from that she wouldn't dare to put her nose into any civilised port where there was a properly equipped workshop.'

Proceeding with the examination, it was eventually decided that while at a proper service station the machine might be made airworthy, situated as they were nothing they could do would achieve that object, even if fuel was available.

'I'm afraid there's nothing else we can do except wait,' announced Biggles. 'Algy should find us when the weather clears. The thing I'm most afraid of is, if he goes to Corbie Island looking for us he may get what we got. With both machines grounded the outlook would begin to look dim.'

'Very dim,' muttered Ginger. He started as from no great distance came a splintering crash. 'What the deuce was that?' he demanded.

'Two 'bergs colliding, I imagine,' returned.
Biggles. 'Or else...' He broke off and looked hard at the ice on which they were standing.

'Or else what?' inquired Ginger anxiously.

'Or else it was a big 'berg breaking up,' said Biggles quietly. 'This ice is damp. It's giving. We must be drifting north.'

'And the fog is lifting,' asserted Ginger. 'Look – there's another 'berg. And there's...' He broke, staring.

There was no need to say more. The fog was, in fact, lifting, so that other 'bergs could be seen. But it was not ice that had so suddenly frozen Ginger's tongue. It was the whaler. Fog-bound like themselves, the ship lay hove-to less than a mile away.

'Quick,' snapped Biggles. 'Get out of sight.'

They moved swiftly, but even so they were too late. A shout from the whaler came eerily over the dark water.

'They've seen us,' said Biggles.

'They've seen us all right,' declared Ginger bitterly. 'They're lowering a boat. What are we going to do about it?'

Biggles shrugged. 'There's nothing we can do about it. We can't fight a whole ship's company and it would be silly to try. Funny thing, I clean forgot the whaler. I suppose there's nothing remarkable about her turning up here. They'll have seen the aircraft so they'll know who we are. Well, it will be interesting to see just who is running the ship.'

'A lot of good that'll do us, if they follow their usual practice of bumping off anyone who gets in their way.'

'Ah well, we shall see,' murmured Biggles.

The whaler's life-boat forged on towards the 'berg under the impetus of six oars. Two men sat in the stern. Both wore navy blue reefer jackets over grey sweaters. On their heads were peaked caps bearing weather-faded gold badges. One, an elderly, heavily built man, with a broad flattish face in which were deeply set, small, calculating eyes, held the tiller. His companion was a different type. He was tall. His face was thin and colourless, and set in such hard lines that it might have been carved out of grey granite. His eyes, pale blue, were on the castaways.

Biggles walked slowly to the edge of the ice and waited. 'They're Nazis all right,' he said in a low voice to Ginger, who stood with him watching the oncoming boat. 'Just look at those faces, and those square heads. I've never been able to decide whether Nazis are born with something in their mentality that gives them faces like that, or whether it is something they acquire.'

'What does it matter, anyway?' growled Ginger. 'They look as though they had never laughed in their lives.'

'They probably haven't,' murmured Biggles.

The side of the boat grated gently against the ice. The rowers shipped their oars. Two jumped ashore and held the boat while the two officers in the stern got out. Both carried automatics. The heavily built man, from his manner obviously the senior, eyed Biggles with a sort of grim satisfaction.

'So!' he exclaimed.

'So what?' inquired Biggles. 'Why the armament?'

The Nazi did not answer. His eyes lifted and surveyed the aircraft. 'So!' he said again.

'It is them,' said his companion, speaking in German.

The other walked on slowly towards the aircraft. The two sailors who had come ashore picked up rifles that had been lying in the boat and motioned to the castaways that they were to follow. Presently all six came to a halt a short distance from the machine.

'Anyone would think they'd never seen a plane before,' breathed Ginger.

'It isn't that, it's merely that they have a pretty good idea that they've seen this one before,' returned Biggles.

Without haste the burly man turned and addressed Biggles in fair English. His voice was harsh and his manner domineering. 'What you do here?' he demanded.

'We were waiting to be picked up,' answered Biggles. 'We had a forced landing.'

'What brought you to these waters?'

'My own business.'

'Ah! And what was that?'

'Suppose I ask some questions?' retorted Biggles. 'What ship is that out there? Who are you? And what are German naval officers doing on a ship of the Norwegian Mercantile Marine?'

'My name is Thom, Lieutenant Thom,' was the answer. 'That may mean something to you?' The German eyed Biggles quizzically as if to note the effect of his words. 'The Norwegian ship you speak of has been taken over by the German Navy.'

'You've heard, of course, that the war is over?' queried Biggles evenly.

'That is where you are wrong,' was the curt reply. 'For some of us the war will never be over. Heil Hitler.'

'That war-cry is out of date, even in Germany,' said Biggles.

The German walked over until he stood within a yard of Biggles, facing him. 'What were you here looking for?' he asked.

'I've found what I was looking for,' returned Biggles softly.

Without warning, without the slightest hint of what he intended, the German's left arm flew out like a piston rod straight into Biggles's stomach. The blow was followed by another, from the right fist. It took Biggles in the face with a vicious smack and stretched him on his back on the ice. He lay still. Blood flowed from his nose across his face to make a little pool on the ice.

'You swine,' rasped Ginger. He made a dash at the German, but one of the sailors caught him by the arm and swung him round.

Thom laughed unpleasantly. His manner was easy and confident. He spoke to one of his men, jerking his head towards the aircraft.

Ginger went to Biggles, took his handkerchief from his pocket and wiped the blood from his face. He was still doing this when he was jerked roughly to his feet by the collar. Looking round he saw that the aircraft was in flames. Thom laughed again. The party began to move towards the boat, which was still waiting at the edge of the ice. Biggles, still unconscious, was dragged along by the jacket, and at the end bundled into the bottom of the boat. Ginger was pushed in.

The fog closed in again as the boat was rowed towards its parent ship, and Ginger reflected bitterly on the evil luck that had caused it to lift at such an untimely moment. The boat was guided to its objective by frequent hails. The prisoners were taken aboard and locked in a reasonably decent cabin. Soon afterwards the timbers vibrated as the engines were started, and at the same time Biggles opened his eyes.

He looked at Ginger and said, 'Where are we, on the whaler?'

Ginger nodded. 'That swine Thom hit you as dirty a blow as ever I saw.'

Biggles sat up, feeling his face tenderly. 'He's a Nazi,' he said simply. 'You must expect Nazis to do that sort of thing, just as you'd expect a mad dog to bite.'

'Are you all right?' asked Ginger anxiously.

'No bones broken, anyway,' answered Biggles, standing up and testing his limbs. 'Don't worry. We haven't finished yet. With any luck at all I'll hand back to Mr. Thom what he gave me – with interest. What's happening?'

'Nothing, except that the ship is under way moving dead slow on account of the fog, I suppose.'

'Bound for Corbie Island, no doubt. We should soon know whether or not I hit the U-boat.'

'Von Schonbeck isn't going to greet you with open arms if he guesses it was you who dropped those depth-charges.'

'From what we know of von Schonbeck he wouldn't greet anyone with open arms, not even his dying mother,' returned Biggles, moistening his bruised lips. Borrowing

Ginger's handkerchief he dipped it in a can of water and bathed his face.

'Thom evidently guessed what we were after,' offered Ginger.

'Bound to. What else would we be doing here but looking for him? I should say these pirates have got the situation pretty well weighed up. One thing they may not guess is that we have a spare machine.'

'Algy will wonder what has happened to us.'

'He may find out. Let us hope so. He's our trump card. Better not talk about him, though, in case anyone comes eavesdropping.'

'Sure you're not hurt?'

Biggles smiled faintly. 'Those two punches shook me up a bit,' he admitted. 'They'd have shaken anyone. I wasn't ready. I shall be all right presently – a couple of black eyes and a bit stiff in the tummy, maybe.' He sat down on one of the two bunks. 'We might as well make ourselves comfortable until we get to where we're going.'

'You think Thom is going to make contact with von Schonbeck?'

'I'm pretty sure of it. He wouldn't have bothered about taking us with him unless he was due to meet a superior officer. He'd have left us on that ice-floe, stiff – or heaved us into the water. Did you see anything as we came aboard?'

'Some sailors.'

'Did any of them look like Norwegians?'

Ginger shook his head. 'Couldn't say. They didn't speak. Just stood watching.'

'We shall soon know,' murmured Biggles, stretching himself on the bunk.

'They took our guns,' said Ginger.

'They wouldn't be likely to overlook a simple precaution like that,' returned Biggles drily. 'Not that guns would be much use to us now. Brains are the only things that'll get us out of this jam. There's this about it. We're not rushed for time. We're a long way from Corbie Island, if that's our destination. At the rate we shall travel through this ice region we shan't arrive much before dawn. That'll give us time to think things over.'

It was, in fact, in the grey light of dawn that the whaler arrived at a landfall which, watching through a porthole, Biggles recognised as Corbie Island. As he expected, the ship turned into the cove where the submarine had been moored. With what interest he watched to see if the U-boat was still there can be imagined. For a little while, as the whaler was coaxed in, travelling dead slow, he had reason to hope that he had sent the U-boat to the bottom with his depth-charges, for he could not see it – at least, at its original mooring. Then, to his intense disappointment, he made out the long, grey shape hard against the rocks farther in the cove. It was movement and sounds of human activity that revealed the submarine's new berth, for the vessel had been so cleverly camouflaged that it was almost impossible to distinguish it from the rocks to which it was made fast. He noticed that rocks had even been strewn along the iron deck in such a way that it would be practically impossible to spot the submarine from the air, even from a low-flying aircraft. Indeed, as the whaler drew near he observed that it was against air observation in particular that the U-boat had been camouflaged. And presently he noticed something else. The submarine was not on an even keel. Her knife-like bows were too far out of the water. This, he thought, could hardly be accidental. It was more likely, he decided, that the vessel had been damaged and was now being repaired – a supposition that was supported by activity around her. All this information he passed back to Ginger as the whaler glided on to an anchorage some sixty or seventy yards from the U-boat. He saw Thom go ashore, to be met by a man in naval uniform who now emerged from a small rock-built structure. It was still too dark to distinguish features or badges of rank, and in any case the newcomer had his coat collar turned up against the biting wind; but he had no doubt as to who it was.

'Von Schonbeck is here,' he told Ginger. 'The next few minutes should be quite exciting.'

He watched Thom and his captain while they stood for a short time in earnest conversation. Then Thom returned to the whaler.

'This, I fancy, is it,' Biggles told Ginger.

His suspicions were confirmed when a minute later footsteps sounded in the gangway outside the cabin. The door was thrown open. Thom stood there, with two sailors armed with rifles.

'This way,' he ordered.

The party made its way to the deck where a number of sailors stood by to watch the little procession. Biggles noticed that they stood in two groups, and he thought he could guess the reason. One party were Germans, originally members of the U-boat's crew, for they were all dressed alike in the usual heavy trousers and sweaters worn by the crews of underwater-craft. Those comprising the other group, a smaller group, from their nondescript garments were ordinary sailors, probably Norwegians, the surviving members of the whaling-ship's company. Their expressions were different from those of the Germans. On their faces could be perceived such emotions as sympathy, commiseration and encouragement. However, neither Germans nor Norwegians spoke as the party descended the ladder that had been lowered and entered a small boat which was rowed quickly to the shore.

The man whom the prisoners had every reason to suppose was von Schonbeck stood waiting. He was younger than Biggles had imagined. Much younger, in fact. He might have been twenty-five years of age, not more, and as far as actual features were concerned no fault could be found. But here again, in the truculent bearing, the cold, humourless face and the hard, merciless mouth, Biggles recognised the typical Hitler fanatic. As he had on more than one occasion remarked to Ginger, they all appeared to have been cast in the same mould – as in fact, in a way, they were.

The party assembled, von Schonbeck lost no time in coming to the point. Considering Biggles with frosty hostility he said in good English, 'You know who I am?'

Biggles answered, 'I think so. You're von Schonbeck, aren't you?'

'Captain von Schonbeck is my name,' was the brittle rejoinder. 'Of the German Navy.'

'There is no German Navy,' reminded Biggles quietly.

'I am an officer of the German Navy,' rasped von Schonbeck.

'There is no such thing,' returned Biggles coolly. 'You may be on the high seas under arms, but that only makes you a common pirate.'

Von Schonbeck drew a deep breath and changed the subject. He jerked a thumb towards the U-boat. 'Are you the man who did this?' he inquired, with anger hardening his voice.

'Did what?'

'Damaged my submarine.'

'I tried to sink it, if that's what you mean,' returned Biggles calmly. 'It's some comfort to me to know that I damaged it. I was afraid I'd missed it altogether. I must be out of practice. Is the damage serious?'

Von Schonbeck's cold blue eyes remained on Biggles's face. Into them crept a suspicion of curiosity, as if the prisoner's nonchalant manner puzzled him. 'I was afraid at first that it was,' he said slowly. 'However, my chief engineer assures me that we shall not be delayed more than twenty-four hours.'

'I'll try to do better next time,' promised Biggles.

'There will be no next time,' answered von Schonbeck grimly. 'When I have finished with you, you will be shot.'

Biggles raised his eyebrows. 'Finished with me?'

'No doubt you are wondering why you were brought here?'

'No.' A ghost of a smile crossed Biggles's face. 'I hadn't even given it a thought.'

Von Schonbeck stared hard for a little while. 'There is a confidence in your manner that excites my curiosity,' he admitted.

'It would be still more excited if you knew what I know,' replied Biggles.

'Indeed! Then let us proceed to find out what that is. You will be well advised to answer my questions truthfully. Who sent you out on this errand?'

'What errand?' inquired Biggles blandly.

'Your errand was to find me, was it not?' snapped von Schonbeck, who seemed to be on the way to losing his temper.

'As a matter of fact it was,' admitted Biggles.

'Who sent you?'

'The British Government.'

'Ah! How did the British Government learn that I was coming here?'

'You'd be surprised if you knew how much they do know about you.'

Von Schonbeck's mouth set in even harder lines. The corners came down. 'Very interesting,' he grated. 'How did your government get this information?'

'That, I'm afraid, I shall have to leave you to find out from some other source.'

'Be careful not to drive me too far.'

'From what I know of you, von Schonbeck, you need no driving to do anything – and as that includes murder you can't go much further,' said Biggles evenly.

The Nazi stared. For a few seconds he seemed to be at a loss for words. Then, with an obvious effort, he recovered his composure. 'So you don't feel inclined to talk, eh?'

Biggles shook his head. 'Not at the moment, and when I do I like to choose my company. But isn't it rather cold standing here? We've had no breakfast, you know.'

At this juncture Thom broke into a spate of words, as if he could no longer contain his fury, but von Schonbeck silenced him with a gesture. Not for a moment did he take his eyes from Biggles's face. 'You are what you English would call a cool customer,' he remarked. 'But that won't

96

help you now,' he added. 'What other ships, if any, are looking for me?'

'I can well understand how anxious you must be to know that, but you can't seriously expect me to tell you,' rejoined Biggles.

'It would make things easier for you if you changed your mind,' suggested the Nazi.

'I doubt it,' murmured Biggles sceptically.

Again von Schonbeck hesitated. 'I'll give you a little while to think it over. I realise, of course, that you must find your present position vexatious.'

Biggles shrugged. 'Please yourself. For the moment my time is yours. But if you must keep us hanging about I'd appreciate some coffee.'

'I'll see that you get some,' promised von Schonbeck. Turning to Thom he went on, in German, 'Take them back to the ship. I'll talk to them again later.'

The prisoners were returned to their cabin, where soon afterwards, sure enough, the coffee arrived – coffee, biscuits and a small tin of butter. The man who brought these refreshments departed, locking the door behind him.

'Von Schonbeck isn't such a bad sort after all,' remarked Ginger, pouring the coffee.

'Pah! Don't let yourself be taken in by this boloney,' muttered Biggles. 'Make no mistake, von Schonbeck hates the sight of us. No doubt he always did hate anything British, but now we've beaten Germany he must hate us with a hate you and I could scarcely understand. He'll shoot us when it suits him. The only reason we aren't stiff now is because we possess information he must be desperately anxious to have. He wants to know how much we know, and what steps the British Government have taken to round him up. Upon that information his life depends and he jolly well knows it. He's put us here while he thinks of a trick to wheedle the information out of us – either that or he hopes we'll lose our nerve and squeal. I'm not complaining. That suits me fine, because it gives us more time to find a way out of this jam.'

'And it gives Algy a little more time—'

'*Ssh!*' Biggles raised a warning hand, glancing at the door. 'I wouldn't talk about that now,' he said softly. 'They may be listening. We'll confine this conversation to things that don't matter. If you have anything to say that does matter, whisper it.'

'How long is this going on do you think?' asked Ginger.

'Not long. Until tonight perhaps, or tomorrow morning. Remember what von Schonbeck said about the damage. His engineer said it would delay the sub for twenty-four hours. I take that to mean if she hadn't been damaged she'd be away by now. It also means that as soon as the sub is ready to travel she'll go. That's when the showdown, so far as we are concerned, will come. Meanwhile, let's keep an eye open through that porthole to see what happens ashore. We may learn something.'

CHAPTER X

Algy Carries On

Meanwhile Algy and Bertie were having an adventure of their own.

After sighting the bears, from which they drew natural but quite wrong conclusions, they did not stay long on the iceberg. There was inevitably a brief debate as to what course they should pursue, for Bertie could see no point in returning to Corbie Island after having drawn blank there earlier in the day. But Algy was not so convinced by this line of argument, pointing out that if Biggles had been shelled by the submarine he must have been pretty close to it, in which case von Schonbeck would take every possible precaution to hide his ship from air observation. This, at Corbie Island, would not be difficult, he averred. He was therefore in favour of making another, a closer inspection of the island, and the water surrounding it.

In the end a compromise was reached. In any case it would be necessary to return to Kerguelen for more petrol before going to Corbie Island. So it was decided that they should make a reconnaissance of all the icebergs in the region, for which they had sufficient fuel, on the off-chance of finding Biggles and Ginger. Failing in this they would return to Kerguelen for petrol and then, conditions permitting, make another trip to Corbie Island. This settled, the aircraft was taken into the air and the survey of the ice-floes begun.

It was a dismal business, for while not admitting it neither entertained any real hope of finding anything of interest. Visibility was far from good, but it might have been worse, although even in bright sunshine the scene would not have induced high spirits. On all sides lay a restless ocean of dark, cold-looking water, dotted by 'bergs, floes and fragments of ice of all shapes and sizes. The picture was one of utter desolation. Apart from an occasional seal there was no sign of life.

For half an hour Algy maintained his patrol, flying in wide circles, examining each piece of ice methodically but without result. Arriving at the extremity of the ice he turned towards Kerguelen with the disconsolate remark: 'No use.'

'Better have a look at that odd 'berg, old boy – the big fellow over there,' suggested Bertie, pointing to a solitary mass of ice that floated a little apart from the main field.

'Okay,' agreed Algy, without enthusiasm. He was bringing the machine round in a shallow turn when he saw something that caused him – to use his own expression – to stiffen on the stick. From behind a rugged pyramid of ice piled up in the middle of the 'berg had appeared a figure – the figure of a man.

'There's one of them!' shouted Bertie.

As Algy flew, now with the nose of the aircraft well down, a second figure appeared and joined the first. Another followed, and another and another, until by the time the 'berg was reached five men stood staring upward. With one accord they waved.

'Good Lord!' ejaculated Bertie. 'What do you make of that?'

'I don't know,' answered Algy slowly. 'They may be some of von Schonbeck's men,' he added cautiously.

'Go nearer,' suggested Bertie. 'They can't hurt us.'

Algy went lower. 'I don't see any ship,' he muttered. 'There's something mighty queer about this. Who on earth are they, and how did they get there?'

'Let's ask them – what?' suggested Bertie cheerfully.

Algy flew lower over the little group, tilting a wing so that he could get a clear view. Upon this the men waved more vigorously, making beckoning signs that could only mean they were anxious for the machine to land.

'I'm going to risk it,' decided Algy, and after making another turn put the machine down on the water to finish its run not far from the ice. The five men came scrambling towards it.

Algy opened the cockpit cover and stood up. 'Who are you?' he shouted.

'Sailors,' was the answer, spoken in English with a pronounced foreign accent. 'Norwegian sailors.'

'Good Lor'! They must be part of the crew of the whaler,' declared Bertie.

'I think you're right,' answered Algy. 'All the same, keep your gun handy in case it's a trap.' He taxied on, slowly, until he was almost within touching distance of the ice. 'Who speaks English?' he inquired.

A tall young fellow with blue eyes and long flaxen hair held up a hand. 'I speak,' he announced.

'Who are you and what are you doing here?' demanded Algy.

'I am Axel Prinz. We are sailors from Norwegian whaling ship,' was the answer. 'Our ship is taken by submarine pirates. She goes away and we are left on ice.'

In view of what he knew Algy found this explanation so feasible that he hesitated no longer. He threw a line ashore. As soon as it was caught and held he stepped on the ice, followed by Bertie.

It did not take the Norwegian who spoke English very long to tell his story. In effect, it amounted to this. With rifles and binoculars he and his four companions had gone off in a small boat to hunt for seals on the floes. This was three days ago. While they were some distance from their ship they had seen an astonishing sight. A submarine had appeared. It had fired a shot at the whaler, forcing the ship to heave-to. The whaler had then been boarded by men from the submarine. There was shooting. Bodies, or what from a distance looked like bodies, had been thrown overboard. Then the submarine and the whaler had sailed away together. That was all. The five men, unable to do anything, had been left behind, and they had, in fact, abandoned all hope of being picked up when they heard the drone of the aircraft. What the submarine was doing – indeed, what the whole affair was about – they had not the remotest idea.

Algy, sympathising with their plight, told them as much as he thought necessary. While not divulging its purpose in those waters he explained that the submarine was a Nazi raider. He also told of the discovery of the two dead Norwegians on Kerguelen Island, information which was received by the sailors with sorrow and anger.

'But the war is over!' cried a grizzled old man, who evidently could speak some English.

'There are still Nazis who do not think so,' answered Algy.

'Pah! These Nazis!' The old man spat his contempt.

'I say, you know, what are we going to do with these chaps?' Bertie asked Algy.

'Obviously, we can't leave them here,' replied Algy. 'The only thing we can do is take them to Kerguelen. They'll be all right there until a ship comes to take them off.'

'Where's your boat?' Algy asked Axel, looking round for it.

'It was crushed in ice during the fog, or we should have tried to reach Kerguelen,' was the answer.

'Have you seen anything more of the submarine or the whaler since they went off?' asked Algy, on the off-chance that they had. 'I ask because we've lost some members of our party, too,' he added.

To his surprise Axel had a lot more to say about this than he expected. In fact, the conclusion of the young Norwegian's story threw a new light on the entire situation. He asserted that on the previous evening the whaler was observed coming back. They thought, naturally, that it was coming to pick them up. Then a fog had blotted out the scene. Soon afterwards an aeroplane was heard in the distance. The engines stopped and they thought it had landed. Later the fog lifted for a little while, and through the binoculars they saw the whaler again. It was a long way off. They watched it lower a boat, which went to a nearby iceberg. They could not see what happened on the 'berg, but presently a great cloud of smoke went up as if a big fire had been lit. The boat was returning to the whaler when the fog came down again and they saw no more.

To this enlightening recital Algy and Bertie listened with mixed emotions of relief and consternation.

'Things are not as bad as we thought, but they're bad enough,' said Algy to Bertie. 'The whole thing is plain enough now. Biggles went to Corbie. The machine was hit by gunfire and came down near the ice. The Nazis on the whaler spotted it. They picked up Biggles and Ginger, set fire to the machine and went off.'

'That doesn't explain the blood,' Bertie pointed out.

'There must have been fighting, and I can well understand that,' said Algy.

'The question is, where has the whaler taken them?'

'To meet von Schonbeck, I should say,' answered Algy. 'That means Corbie Island, unless they have a rendezvous on the open sea, which doesn't strike me as very likely.'

Bertie looked worried. 'But I say, old boy, what are we going to do about it?'

'That will need thinking about,' returned Algy. 'It looks as if my hunch about Corbie Island is right. That's where we shall finish up, I fancy, sooner or later. But the first thing is to get these chaps to Kerguelen. They must be in need of a hot meal.'

'It's going to be a bit of a squash, if we try to pack them in for one hop,' opined Bertie dubiously.

'We can manage it,' declared Algy. 'We haven't far to go. Let's get them aboard. There's no point in hanging about here any longer. We'll keep an eye open for the whaler as we go. We shall need more petrol in the tanks before we start anything.'

The Norwegians were squeezed into the machine. Squeezed is the only word. But the machine had plenty of reserve power, and once in the air made no difficulty of its extra load.

On the run to Kerguelen Algy devoted his attention to the problem that now confronted him. He knew that strictly speaking Biggles would wish him to proceed with the original quest, regardless of personal consideration. This, eventually, he was prepared to do, but for the moment he had no intention of ignoring Biggles's predicament. That, in his heart, came first. The gold could wait. If Biggles and the gold could be collected together, and this he thought was just within the bounds of possibility, so well and good. The first place to explore, he decided, was Corbie Island, but it was now clear that if the whaler or the submarine was there, a direct landing and a frontal attack was out of the question. Still, there were other ways, and by the time he had put the machine down at its Kerguelen base he had well turned them over in his mind.

In the hut he put the matter before Bertie and his new allies, whom he felt were now personally concerned in the affair in that they had comrades to avenge and a ship to recover. He talked while the Norwegians consumed a satisfying meal, prepared by one of their party who happened to be the whaler's cook. Algy announced his intention of visiting Corbie Island. It would be rash, if not futile, he asserted, to attempt this in daylight, but it might be done at night. The island was several miles long so it should be possible to effect a landing without being seen or heard. There would be a long walk to the cove which he suspected was the anchorage used by the submarine, but that couldn't be avoided.

Axel now made a statement which made it clear that the Norwegians were likely to be more helpful than Algy had supposed. In the first place they knew Corbie Island quite well, having landed there several times on previous voyages for fresh water and the wild cabbages that grew there. And they still had the guns which they had taken with them on their sealing expedition. So it seemed that they would be useful both as guides and as fighting allies. Not only were they willing to take part in an expedition, but they were burning to go, to redress their wrongs. This suited Algy very well and he expressed his satisfaction.

'All right,' he concluded. 'You fellows have a rest and a clean up while I'm getting the machine ready. We'll start at sundown, weather permitting.'

CHAPTER XI

Cut and Thrust

Biggles and Ginger, from their cabin prison in the whaler, had seen plenty to occupy their minds and provide them with subjects for conversation. A great noise of hammering and banging came from the submarine, and a party of men could be seen working in a cradle slung over the stern. Others worked from a small boat, evidently part of the U-boat's equipment.

'It looks as if I got a near miss close to her rudder, which may have affected her steering gear,' said Biggles thoughtfully.

The next thing that happened was the warping of the whaler flush against a low cliff, where she was quickly and cleverly camouflaged with netting of a nature and colour which called from Biggles a remark that it must have been specially designed for the locality.

'The Germans always were thorough in little things,' he observed, with grudging admiration. 'This is a really clever job. Von Schonbeck is taking no chances. We're well covered against air reconnaissance – and so, I see, is the submarine. It would take a wizard to see anything here except rock and water.'

'Maybe it's a good thing for us,' said Ginger. 'We should look silly if Algy came over, spotted the whaler or the submarine, and handed out a couple of depth-charges.'

'Algy may come, but unless von Schonbeck is fool enough to reveal his position by opening fire, I doubt if he will see us,' returned Biggles.

'You don't think von Schonbeck will open fire?' queried Ginger.

'Not unless he has reason to suppose that he has been spotted. There isn't much point in hiding a target and then giving the position away by taking offensive action. If von Schonbeck is half as clever as he is reputed to be he won't make that blunder.'

Confirmation of this was soon provided. The drone of aero engines announced the approach of an aircraft, which those in the cabin knew could only be their reserve machine.

'Here comes Algy,' said Biggles quietly. 'We shall soon see how it goes.'

On the submarine, in response to a whistle, all movement ceased after the workers had dived for cover. The aircraft came on. All remained still. Gulls drifted languidly over the scene. The aircraft circled, and at length disappeared from the vision of the watchers. Its receding drone told them that it was retiring.

'They didn't spot us,' said Biggles. 'If they had they would have hung around for a bit, even if they didn't take action.'

The work on the submarine was resumed. The day wore on. Later, a parade of men was held on a level area of rock. Both von Schonbeck and Thom were present. Some of the men were issued with picks and shovels.

Biggles counted fifteen men in all. 'I wonder what all this is about?' he questioned, as the party, after turning with military precision, marched off and was soon lost to sight.

More time passed. Work on the submarine was continued. The prisoners were served with a plain meal. Biggles continued to watch through the porthole. Suddenly he gave a low whistle. 'Take a look at this,' he invited.

Ginger, who was reclining on a bunk, joined him, and saw four men staggering along carrying an oblong wooden box obviously of considerable weight. It was deposited on a rock near the submarine's conning tower.

'What the deuce is it?' queried Ginger.

'I'll give you two guesses – and you ought to be right each time,' answered Biggles. 'The picks and shovels should have told us what was afoot.'

'I still don't get it,' muttered Ginger.

'Have you forgotten what brought von Schonbeck here – and us, too, if it comes to that?'

Enlightenment dawned in Ginger's eyes. He drew a deep breath. 'The gold!' he burst out.

'That's a bullion box those fellows are carrying,' Biggles told him.

'They're digging it out and getting ready to load up.'

'That's what it looks like,' agreed Biggles.

'And we're stuck here and can't do anything about it.'

'Not a thing,' agreed Biggles again. 'Here comes another lot.'

A second party of four men came into sight carrying a box similar to the first. The original four were on their way back. As the two parties passed some joke was evidently exchanged, for there was laughing.

'They seem to be happy,' growled Ginger.

'So would anyone be with five million pounds to spend,' said Biggles, smiling.

'You seem to be taking all this pretty lightly,' remarked Ginger, looking hard at Biggles.

Biggles shrugged. 'Moaning won't get us anywhere, will it? The sub still has a long way to go.'

The work ashore proceeded without hitch, both on the submarine and with the transportation of the gold. The stack of boxes near the U-boat grew steadily in size. Eventually, von Schonbeck and Thom reappeared.

'I should say that's the lot,' said Biggles.

Towards evening there was a further burst of activity. The cradle over the submarine's stern was drawn up and the camouflage removed. After everything had been made shipshape von Schonbeck and Thom went aboard.

'Now what?' asked Ginger. 'Don't tell me they're going to move off?'

'The gold is still ashore. They wouldn't be likely to go without it,' answered Biggles dryly.

Soon afterwards the meaning of this latest manoeuvre was made clear. The U-boat's engines were started and the vessel moved out to open water. One or two turns were made, after which she returned to her mooring.

'They've tested her,' said Biggles. 'Apparently she's all right.'

'Which means she'll push off.'

'Not necessarily. They've got to load and stow that gold, and that will take some time. By the time they've done that it will be dark. Of course, von Schonbeck may decide to go right away, but on the other hand he may prefer to wait for daylight before taking his ship through that narrow channel to the open sea. He's got the whaler to dispose of, anyway. I don't suppose he'll leave it here.'

Nightfall put an end to further observation. When darkness closed in the gold was still lying on the rock, which, as Biggles remarked, tended to confirm his opinion that von Schonbeck intended to wait for morning before taking his ship out to the open sea. And the fact that only a sailor came to the cabin, bringing more food for the prisoners, supported this view.

'Yes, it looks as though they're going to spend another night here,' asserted Biggles. 'That suits us as well as anything. It gives us a bit more time, anyway.'

'A bit more time for what?'

'Oh, anything,' said Biggles nonchalantly.

'You think Algy might come back?'

Biggles considered the question. 'He might. We've no real reason for supposing that he will, though. And even if he does it's hard to see what he can do.'

'That's cheerful,' muttered Ginger.

'Unfortunately, my lad, it's the truth – and it's always as well to face up to facts. Dawn tomorrow will be zero hour – as far as we're concerned, anyway.'

After that they fell silent. There was nothing they could do except lie on their bunks. After a while, Biggles's steady breathing told Ginger that he was asleep.

At some time he, too, must have fallen asleep, although just when that happened he could not remember. But he was awakened by heavy footsteps outside the door, and the turning of the handle.

Biggles, who was already up, threw him a glance. 'This, I should say, is it,' he said quietly.

The door was opened and Thom, an expression of malevolent satisfaction on his face, stood on the threshold. He beckoned to Biggles with a peremptory finger. 'Come,' he ordered.

Ginger, thinking naturally that he was included in this invitation, moved towards the door, but with a harsh 'I did not say you,' Thom thrust him back with unnecessary violence.

Anger tightened Ginger's lips and set his nostrils quivering, but Biggles caught his eye and shook his head so slightly that the movement was almost imperceptible. 'Put your hackles down,' he said softly. 'It won't help matters. So long – in case.'

With that Biggles was bundled out of the cabin. The door was slammed and locked, leaving Ginger alone inside. He strode to the porthole, through which the bleak grey light of dawn was filtering.

Biggles realised that he was being taken ashore, to von Schonbeck, for the interview which had been promised, and the reception that awaited him as he stepped ashore near the U-boat left him in no doubt as to the finality of its nature. The gold boxes, he noted, were no longer there. In their place stood a file of six sailors who eyed the prisoner with hostile curiosity. Each man carried a rifle and wore a cartridge belt. At a short distance von Schonbeck was waiting, legs apart, service cap at a jaunty angle, a cigar between his teeth, hands thrust deep into the pockets of his short blue coat. Biggles smiled cynically, realising that he had been marched past what was obviously a firing party for no other purpose than intimidation.

'We are about to move off,' greeted von Schonbeck affably. 'Have you considered my proposition?'

'There was nothing to consider,' returned Biggles briefly.

The Nazi's expression did not change. He tapped the ash from his cigar. 'I am trying to give you a chance for your life,' he announced.

Biggles raised his eyebrows. 'I should never have guessed it.'

'I mean what I say.'

Biggles shook his head sadly. 'Even if I could accept the word of a Nazi – and the events of the war have shown what a flimsy thing that is – I would tell you nothing,' he said quietly. 'Go ahead. Do what you like. The only thing I have to say to you, von Schonbeck, is this. You still have a long way to go.'

'It may be that your young friend could be more easily persuaded,' said von Schonbeck thoughtfully.

'Try, if you like, but I think you'd be wasting your time,' opined Biggles.

'Ah well.' Von Schonbeck sighed – or pretended to sigh. 'You British always did have a reputation for being pig-headed. You'll see where that will get you at the end.'

'Your own methods during the war can hardly be described as overwhelmingly successful,' returned Biggles, a suspicion of a sneer creeping into his voice.

The thrust went home. The German scowled. 'This is not a good moment to remind me of that,' he rasped. 'When this affair is over there will be one damned Britisher the less, anyhow.' Von Schonbeck paused, and with an effort checked his rising temper. 'But to argue about things that are past at a time like this is folly,' he went on. 'Now then, as one officer and gentleman to another—'

Biggles looked incredulous. 'As *what*? An officer and gentleman? God save us. Von Schonbeck, you're just a cheap, cold-blooded murderer, high on the list of war criminals. Very soon every newspaper in the world will carry the story of your crimes, your butchery of helpless women and unarmed seamen. You may shoot me, and since a hyena can't change its coat I'm sure that was always your intention. But, believe me, I'd sooner go out here and now than live another twenty years with a reputation like yours. They'll put your photo in the papers, and every decent seaman between the Arctic and the Antarctic will spit when he looks at it. That should leave you in no doubt as to what I think of you.'

Thom took a swift pace forward and struck Biggles across the face with his open hand.

Von Schonbeck, whose face had flamed scarlet, laughed harshly. 'What you think of me is of no import- ance,' he grated. 'It is what I am going to do to you that will count.'

'Go ahead,' invited Biggles.

Von Schonbeck barked an order. Two men seized Biggles by the arms and jostled him forward a little way until he stood with his back against a face of rock. Another order and the firing party lined up in front of him. Another order and they came to attention.

'Would you like a bandage over your eyes?' sneered von Schonbeck.

'No,' answered Biggles evenly. 'There's nothing a Nazi can give me that I can't take.'

Von Schonbeck raised his hand.

'Take aim,' Thom ordered his men.

The rifles of the firing party came to their shoulders. The crash of an explosion shattered the silence. Biggles stumbled and fell flat.

CHAPTER XII

Ginger Starts Something

Now while Biggles was taking what he had good reason to suppose would be his last view of the earth from the inhospitable rock of the island, Ginger, still secure in the whaler, was nearer than ever before to panic. Watching through the porthole he saw Biggles taken ashore, saw von Schonbeck standing there, saw the firing squad and guessed its purpose. Yet there was nothing he could do. Absolutely nothing. He tried to do something, of course. In sheer despair he wrenched at the door handle, kicked the door and tore at the metal frame of the porthole, although he knew that these efforts were silly and futile. His only comfort – a poor crumb of comfort indeed – was the thought, 'I shall be next.'

At this juncture, while he was still staring ashen-faced through the porthole, a sudden noise behind him brought him round with a nervous start, in such a state of agitation was he. He saw that the door had been opened. A face, a leathery, weather-beaten face, alert with apprehension and anxiety, was peering into the cabin. The eyes met Ginger's. After a furtive glance along the corridor behind him the man made a swift beckoning movement with his hand.

Ginger felt intuitively that this man was a friend. Indeed, his attitude and manner almost proved it. So the question he asked was really automatic. 'Who are you?' he demanded.

'I friend,' was the terse reply. 'Come. Come quick. We go.'

'Go where?'

The man made a gesture of urgency. 'Hide. Germans shoot.'

The man's English was limited, but the words he did use were pregnant with significance. In any case Ginger was in no state to be particular. He was prepared to go anywhere, do anything, if only to get out of the cabin. 'Are you a Norwegian?' he queried, although here again he was pretty sure of his ground.

'Yes, me Norwegian,' was the quick rejoinder. The man laid a finger on his lips. 'Come. Not any noise,' he warned.

Still without knowing exactly what the man intended beyond the obvious fact that he proposed deserting the ship, Ginger followed his new acquaintance into the corridor, along which they passed swiftly to a flight of steps which, as it soon turned out, gave access to the deck near the bows. From this point Ginger made a lightning survey of the ship for possible danger. There were several sailors in sight. All were lining the rail overlooking the shore where a drama was being enacted, their attention riveted on it, as was natural. Ginger's guide, impatient at the brief delay, plucked him by the sleeve, and lifting aside the camouflage netting indicated that they should climb the low cliff against which the ship was moored. But in this simple manner of escape – for it was evident that the Norwegian did not look beyond that – Ginger was not prepared to participate. In point of fact escape was the last thing in his mind. The thought dominant in his brain was how to help Biggles. His eyes were on the shore and he could see clearly enough what was about to happen. The question was, how to stop it, and this was not so clear. The Norwegian was still hanging on the cliff, waiting, so Ginger ran to him and asked him if he had a pistol. Just what he would have done with this weapon had it been available is a matter for conjecture. It seems likely that he would have launched, from long range, a single-handed attack on the firing party, and lost his life for his pains. However, this did not occur for the simple reason that the Norwegian had no pistol. Indeed, he had no weapon of any sort, as he explained by eloquent gestures. Ginger, by this time in a fever of consternation, turned away, and in doing so collided with a weapon the like of which he had never seen before although his common sense told him what it was. It was the heavy harpoon gun, mounted in the bows, by which the whaler slew the great sea beasts for which it was designed. The massive point of a steel harpoon, with hinged barbs, a fearful-looking instrument, projected from the muzzle.

Ginger caught his breath as he realised the possibilities. He had an insane desire to laugh. 'Is this loaded?' he demanded of his companion, who by signs was still imploring him to escape while the opportunity offered.

The man shook his head.

'Where are the shells?' demanded Ginger. 'Quick!'

The man pointed at a stoutly built wooden box, almost the size of a chest, clamped to the deck near the gun.

Ginger threw open the lid and saw rows of enormous cartridges. 'How do you load this thing?' he asked in a hoarse whisper.

The man joined him. 'Are you mad?' he asked with some agitation.

'Yes,' answered Ginger frankly. 'How do I load it?'

The man started to explain, but Ginger, unable to follow his instructions, broke in impatiently. 'Load it.'

The Norwegian, with a deftness obviously the result of long experience, slipped a cartridge into the breech and closed it. 'She is ready,' he said simply. 'She fire when you pull trigger.'

With a sort of delirious joy Ginger grabbed the weapon, swung the muzzle round – for it moved on well-oiled bearings – and took rough aim at the party on the shore. To his horror he saw that the sailors had raised their rifles. His finger coiled round the trigger. With a vicious jerk he pulled it, and then stepped back to watch the result.

There was a violent explosion, much louder than he expected. The harpoon, glinting as it caught the light, flashed a graceful curve through the grey atmosphere. Behind it, sagging slightly, trailed the line to which it was attached. Until this moment Ginger knew nothing of the line. Not that it made any difference.

The harpoon missed the target at which it was aimed by a fairly wide margin, although that is no matter for wonder. It hit the conning tower of the submarine with a metallic clang, glanced off, and spinning wildly whirled on towards the group assembled behind it. Ginger saw Biggles fall flat and for a ghastly moment thought that the harpoon had hit him. Thom spun a good dozen yards and went down screaming. The rope, coiling like a snake in convulsions, threw the firing party into confusion. In actual fact Ginger was not at all sure of what had happened. One thing, however, was certain – he had interrupted the proceedings. Satisfied with his efforts so far he turned to reload the weapon, but the Norwegian clutched him by the arm and shouted to him to run. This, really, was sound advice, but Ginger was in no mood to listen to advice, good or bad.

From then on the affair was chaotic. Shots were fired. By whom, who at, and from where, Ginger had no idea. There was shouting. The old Norwegian was yelling in his own language. The sailors who had been lining the rail had turned, and they, too, shouted as they ran towards the gun, some in German and some in what Ginger supposed to be Norwegian. What is commonly called a free fight started. The old Norwegian picked up an iron spike that lay near the gun and threw it. It struck the leading German in the face and knocked him down. Ginger closed with the second. He went down under his man, who was a good deal heavier, and was getting the worst of it when the body pressing on him went limp. Pulling himself clear he saw a Norwegian swinging a wooden mallet in a sort of frenzy. Everywhere men were fighting, wrestling, some standing, some falling. It was evident that now the revolt had started, now that the Norwegians had turned on their captors, they were wiping out old scores and doing it with gusto.

Ginger took no further part in this particular affair. The melee was too confused, and although for the moment the Norwegians appeared to be more than holding their own, in his heart he felt sure that in the long run they would lose, because they were outnumbered. He was thinking, of course, of the Nazi crew on the U-boat, who, he was certain, would soon be aboard to quell the rising. And thinking on these lines he could find time to be sorry for the disaster which, he supposed, he had brought upon the unarmed whalers. He was anxious, desperately anxious, to learn what had happened to Biggles, and in the hope of ascertaining this he made his way to the rail which commanded a view of the scene ashore. There, an unexpected sight met his gaze. As far as he had been aware there had been no Norwegians on the island, so if there was any fighting at all, he assumed that it would be Biggles against the rest. But this was not so. Another battle, a battle in which firearms were being used, was being waged ashore. Perhaps 'battle' was not the right word. It appeared that a small party of men, Biggles amongst them, was making a fighting withdrawal towards the interior of the island. From here, too, shots were being fired. Ginger could not understand it all. Not that he tried very hard. His chief concern was that Biggles was still on his feet, and seemed to have found some unexpected allies. Where these had come from he could not imagine. It was all very puzzling.

A new factor now appeared on the scene – or rather, over the scene. In a vague sort of way Ginger connected it with the happenings ashore without being able to reach anything definite in the way of understanding. It was the aircraft. It appeared suddenly over the crest of a hill some distance away. Ginger shouted from sheer excitement. A whistle shrilled on the shore, and the Germans who had been pursuing Biggles and his unknown friends began running back to the U-boat. Biggles and his party now turned back and pursued the Germans, who, in response to von Schonbeck's frantic shouting, converged on the U-boat and dived into the conning tower.

The aircraft came on. It still had some distance to travel, however, to the scene of hostilities, and when it did reach them it circled as if the pilot was undecided as to what course to take. This Ginger could well understand. A newcomer to the scene, he realised, would find it hard to sort out the combatants. The result of this hesitation was that by the time the machine reached the cove the submarine was under way, nosing towards the passage to the open sea. From the behaviour of the aircraft Ginger thought that the pilot – Algy or Bertie, he knew not which – had only just spotted the U-boat, but when the pilot did see it he came straight on. A depth-charge came sailing down. Ginger ducked, for the missile seemed to be coming uncomfortably close to the whaler. There was a thundering explosion. Ginger jumped up and saw that the depth-charge, obviously aimed at the U-boat, had missed its mark. It had fallen some distance astern. A quick-firing gun on the deck of the submarine started pouring up flak, forcing the aircraft to take evading action. Nevertheless, dashing in, it sent a second depth-charge hurtling down. Again Ginger ducked, for this one, dropped in haste, looked like coming nearer. Again an explosion thundered, flinging columns of water sky-high. Again Ginger popped up, in time to observe that the shot was another miss. He groaned with disappointment. Then he remembered that the gold was on board the U-boat, a fact of which the pilot of the aircraft must be unaware, and he was glad, in a way, that the submarine looked like getting clear. He had no idea of the depth of the water in the cove, but should it be very deep, and it might well be, there was a good chance that the gold would have been lost for ever.

The U-boat, after rocking dangerously in the tremendous swell set up by the explosion, moved on towards the entrance. The whaler rocked too, so that Ginger was hard put to keep his feet. Spitting flak, the U-boat held on, followed by the aircraft, still taking evading action, the only sensible thing to do in the circumstances, as Ginger realised. The machine took no further offensive action because there was nothing more it could do. It carried no more depth-charges, nor, for that matter, any other weapon powerful enough to impede the progress of the submarine. The *Tarpon's* machine-guns were no use against a steel hull, so the submarine ran on through the channel to the open sea where, after the gunners had retired, it submerged and was lost to view. Not forgetting the gold, Ginger was conscious of a sense of frustration and disappointment.

Still somewhat dazed by the speed of events, and aware that the pandemonium behind him had subsided, he turned to see what had happened. A litter of bodies on the whaler's deck revealed at a glance the fury of the struggle that had been waged. It was equally clear that the whalers had won, for all those still on their feet were Norwegians. The old man with the leathery face – now bloodstained but twisted in a grin of triumph – was there.

Now that the affair on the whaler was over Ginger had no time to spare for it. He was more anxious to make contact with Biggles. So with a shout of congratulations and thanks to the Norwegians he went back to the rail, nearly being hit by a bullet as he did so. Realising that those ashore must be unaware of what had happened on the ship, and that they would naturally suppose it to be in enemy hands, he jumped up and waved his arms, at the same time shouting to call attention to his presence. Out of the corner of his eye he saw the aircraft coming in to land from the direction of the sea, but his attention was really on the shore, where a little knot of men stood together, one of them bending over something that lay on the ground. Biggles was amongst them. He looked across the water at Ginger and waved. He spoke to the men around him, with a result that two of them got into the little boat that had taken him ashore and rowed out to the ship.

Five minutes later Ginger was on the island talking to Biggles. The object on the ground turned out to be Thom. He was not a pretty sight, for the harpoon had gone clean through him.

Ginger shuddered. 'Did I do that?' he asked aghast.

'It was a good shot whoever did it,' declared Biggles. 'Did you fire the gun?'

'I did,' admitted Ginger.

'With more practice you'll be able to go in for whaling when you get too old to fly,' said Biggles. Then he became serious. 'You were just about in time, although at first I thought the harpoon was going to get me. I saw it coming and went flat. But let's get the situation straightened out. What's happened on the ship?'

'The Norwegians took a hand and cleaned up the Nazis,' explained Ginger. 'Where the deuce did these other fellows come from?' He pointed at three more men coming towards the scene. One of them was Algy. 'That means Bertie must have been flying the aircraft,' he concluded.

'Evidently,' replied Biggles. 'I'm still not clear as to what has happened, except that an attack on the Nazi camp was launched just about the time you fired the gun. But here comes Bertie. No doubt he'll tell us all about it.'

The aircraft had taxied up to the rock and Bertie had jumped ashore. He reached the party at the same time as Algy, who was plastered with mud and breathing heavily.

Bertie started when his eyes fell on the mangled remains of Thom. Adjusting his monocle he regarded the spectacle with disgust. 'Here, I say, you know, who made that beastly mess?' he inquired weakly.

'Never mind that,' answered Biggles. 'We're waiting to hear your end of the story.'

'Ask Algy,' pleaded Bertie. 'I'm still all of a dither. Did you see that bally submarine shooting at me? No joke, I can tell you.'

'You needn't tell me,' said Biggles curtly. 'I've had some. Go ahead, Algy.'

Algy explained how he and Bertie had picked up the Norwegians marooned on the ice, had landed at the far end of the island during the hours of darkness, and were getting into position to attack the Nazi camp when the firing of the gun had upset their plan. However, they had pressed on the attack, after which Biggles knew as much about it as they did.

'Well, it seems to have worked out all right,' said Biggles at the finish.

'You're not forgetting that von Schonbeck has got away?' Ginger pointed out bitterly.

'And I'm not forgetting that we've got away, either,' returned Biggles. 'An hour ago I wouldn't have given an empty petrol can for our chance. Von Schonbeck has gone and he's got the gold with him, but he's not home yet; with any luck we'll catch up with him before he gets there. Those cookies of yours, Bertie, were pretty close, and if they haven't loosened some plates I shall be surprised. The best thing we can do is get back to base and talk the thing over. Before we do that, though, we'd better see what we have on our hands here.'

'How about chasing the sub?' suggested Ginger.

Biggles shook his head. 'Not a hope. Von Schonbeck will stay under water for as long as he dares, knowing there's a hostile aircraft about. Not that it would make any difference if we did spot him. We've nothing to hit with.'

'If the U-boat is likely to leave a trail why not follow it?' suggested Ginger.

'What's the use of following a trail if you can't hurt the thing making it?' returned Biggles. 'Even if we had more depth charges, and improved on Bertie's bombing, Raymond wouldn't thank us for sending the gold to Davy Jones. That isn't the idea. And there's no sense in burning petrol for nothing; if we happened to run into a gale it would take us all our time to get home, anyway.'

'We could look and see if the U-boat *is* leaving a trail,' pressed Ginger.

'Take a look at the weather,' invited Biggles. He pointed.

Glancing up Ginger saw black squall clouds racing low across the sky. A rising wind was tearing the surface of the water. 'Okay,' he said in a resigned voice.

A check disclosed that of the original Norwegian crew twelve were still alive, including those who had been picked up on the ice-floe. One had been killed during the fight on the whaler, and three others wounded, although not seriously. One of the shore party had a slight gunshot wound. Of the Nazis, apart from Thom, three had been killed and four wounded. It turned out that the captain of the whaler had been murdered by the Nazis when the ship had been seized, but the first mate was still alive and asserted that he was able to take the ship to port.

'What are we going to do with the prisoners?' asked Algy.

'We certainly can't clutter ourselves up with them,' answered Biggles. 'There seems to be quite a dump here, with food and medical stores, so I think the best thing is to leave them here to look after themselves for the time being. We'll notify Raymond at the first opportunity; no doubt he'll send a ship out to take them off.'

One other point of interest came to light. The whaler, as Biggles suspected, had taken on board most of the reserve oil from the secret base at Kerguelen, the Norwegians explaining that it had been von Schonbeck's intention to use the whaler as a mobile base, and perhaps as a blind to hide his activities. For this purpose he had, as was known, put a Nazi crew on board from his own ship.

'Which means that his own crew must be shrinking,' observed Biggles.

After a short debate the matter was left thus. The Norwegians were to take their vessel to Biggles's base at Kerguelen, from where, after refitting as far as possible and restoring their wounded, they could make their way to their home port of Oslo, to report their version of the affair to their owners and the Norwegian Government. This would leave the airmen free to pursue the U-boat in the remaining aircraft. In the first place, however, they would have to return to base to refuel. They would take up the hunt from there.

'Do you think you will catch these swines?' Axel asked Biggles.

'I think we have a fair chance,' was the reply. 'If our depth-charges have strained some of the U-boat's plates, and that seems likely, she will leave an oil trail that we should have no difficulty in picking up. Once we find the trail we'll play cat and mouse with her until we catch her on the surface.'

'The one snag is,' he told the others later, when they were on board the machine, 'now von Schonbeck has the gold we mustn't sink him if it can be avoided. Of course, now he knows that we're after him he may change his plans. He may give South America a miss and decide on some other hide-out. He has a lot of places to choose from. However, we'll talk about that later.'

He took the machine off and headed for Kerguelen.

CHAPTER XIII

Von Schonbeck Tries Again

Leaving the Norwegians to follow in the whaler in their own time, Biggles set his course for base. There was a delay as the aircraft passed over the area where the U-boat had disappeared, some time being employed in searching for indications of her track. But crested waves were now chasing each other in endless procession across the ocean, and with spindrift flying above them reconnaissance was hopeless and yielded nothing.

'I'm afraid it would need a lot of oil to show on a sea like that,' observed Biggles critically. 'If this weather persists for any length of time we're going to have a tiresome job picking up the trail. We may never find it. In fact, everything may now depend on the weather. It raises another possibility. If the sub is damaged, and if the sea gets worse, she may not be able to ride it out, in which case she'll go to the bottom taking the gold with her and no one will ever know for certain what did happen. That would be a most unsatisfactory end to the story.'

The machine went on to make a somewhat hazardous landing at the Kerguelen base. The water inside the cove was calm enough, but the air above it was tormented by treacherous gusts, due to the rugged nature of the terrain.

In these the aircraft bucked and rocked before sliding down to rest in the sheltered anchorage. The machine was soon made fast, and under Biggles's orders it was refuelled forthwith in case it should be needed in a hurry. The party then retired to the hut for a quick bath and a badly needed meal. While they were eating, from time to time Biggles threw anxious glances at the window and the howling gale that now raged outside.

'It looks like working up for a real snorter,' he remarked. 'It's no earthly use going out in that. We might as well make up our minds to it and settle down to take it easy.'

He was right. The storm persisted, with squalls of hail, sleet, and snow. It raged all that night, all the next day and all the following night. With visibility zero the airmen could do nothing. They were grounded. Biggles spent most of the daylight hours staring out of the window, smoking an endless chain of cigarettes, seldom speaking except to refer to the situation. The others, knowing what the enforced inaction was doing to his nerves, fell quiet. Of course, they, too, felt the strain – or rather, the slackening of the strain and the inevitable reaction.

'What I'd like to know is this,' remarked Biggles once, flicking the ash from his cigarette. 'How much oil had von Schonbeck got aboard when he pushed off? He went in a deuce of a hurry, don't forget. Most of his reserve fuel was in the whaler. He'd need full tanks to make the Magellan Straits – that is, if he's sticking to his original plan. We were on the whaler when she made Corbie Island, and after that we were always on it or near it. I can't recall seeing or hearing anything like refuelling operations. On the other hand, of course, the submarine may have been lying there with full tanks. It's an important point. After running through a sea like this the state of her tanks will play a vital part in the game, because they'll control her endurance range. But there, it's no use guessing. I wonder how the whaler's getting on? Undermanned as she is the crew must be having a pretty thin time out there in that perishing murk, with ice about.'

'I can't help thinking we ought to radio Raymond and tell him the position,' put in Algy, moodily.

'And I can't see that it would do any good,' returned Biggles curtly. 'He's too far away to help us, considering the time factor. If it comes to that we should be no better off if we had a dozen planes here. They'd all be grounded. If von Schonbeck picked up our signal – and you can bet your sweet life he's listening for signals – it might do a lot of harm. It would tell him that we're still on the job and perhaps give him an idea where we're working from – if he doesn't know already. Radio silence will keep him guessing. It's better that way.'

On the morning of the third day the storm blew itself out. The wind dropped to an occasional gust and the sea began to subside. Biggles, his irritation gone, became the very spirit of activity.

'I'm getting off right away, taking Ginger with me,' he announced crisply. 'I don't know when we shall be back. We may be some time. If von Schonbeck has managed to ride out the storm he should be a long way off by now, but he won't be outside our range, I think, because he wouldn't risk running at full speed through a heavy sea. Still, he's an old hand at this game and we shall have to be prepared for tricks – tricks like laying false trails by means of oil barrels with holes punched in them to allow the oil to seep out.' Biggles spoke to Algy. 'When we come back, if we've found nothing you can carry on. If necessary we'll fly complete circles at increasing distances until we do strike the trail.'

'There may not be any trail. The storm may have washed it out,' suggested Algy.

'Maybe. But the sea is down now and if the sub is still travelling she'll be leaving signs which we ought to see as we cut across them. There is this in our favour. There aren't likely to be any other craft about to mislead us.'

'And suppose you find the trail – what then?' inquired Algy.

'I shall follow it,' answered Biggles. 'If the sub is running under water, which is unlikely, or if she dives when she sees us, I shall call up Raymond, pinpoint the position, and ask him to throw a cordon of anti-submarine craft round the whole area. The sub won't be able to sit on the bottom in these waters, they're too deep; and if the engines are running sound detectors should pick them up. Sooner or later the sub will have to surface if only to charge her batteries; and even if von Schonbeck realises that he is being dogged he'll have to carry on because he wouldn't dare to risk running out of fuel. It's a long way to the Magellan Straits. If his tanks dried up he'd be finished. He'd be a mere hulk, a floating tin can with no means of getting anywhere and at the mercy of the first storm that blew along. Diving wouldn't save him. A few near misses with depth-charges would either send him to the bottom or bring him to the surface. But the first thing is to find the submarine. By the way, you fellows keep an eye open for the whaler. It's time she was here. Come on, Ginger.'

Biggles strode down to the machine, which was soon in the air, flying under the usual leaden sky over a sea that still heaved in the aftermath of the recent storm. But the wind had died away and the waves were fast going down.

'In a couple of hours, if there's no more wind, she'll be flat calm,' said Biggles confidently, as he climbed for height. 'I'm setting a course to fly a big arc right across the region between Corbie Island and the Magellan Straits,' he announced. 'Keep your eyes open and tell me if you see anything – anything at all.'

'Okay,' acknowledged Ginger, and the search began.

For more than two hours the *Tarpon* roared on an outward course across a sullen waste of water. Nothing was seen. Absolutely nothing. Not even an iceberg or a solitary whale. Ginger, aware that they were hundreds of miles from home, or, for that matter, from the nearest land, regarded the featureless expanse below with rising apprehension. He could not help remembering that the best aero engines sometimes fail, that they were over the loneliest place on the globe, and, moreover, at about the limit of the range. From his manner Biggles might have been unaware of this. Consequently Ginger drew a deep breath of relief when the nose of the machine began to swing round.

'Queer,' said Biggles. 'Dashed queer. I would have wagered twelve months' pay that the submarine was losing oil. If there was oil we should see it.' This was obviously true, for the sea now lay as tranquil as a pond.

'He may have changed his mind and gone another way,' suggested Ginger.

'Then he must have another oil dump somewhere or he'd never make a landfall,' declared Biggles. 'He's a long way to go, even to South America. I'll try farther out.'

For about twenty minutes Biggles flew on, and then turned for home on an even greater circle than the outward journey. Ginger said nothing but he was far from happy. Biggles was taking chances, which was not like him. They were cutting the petrol supply fine, even in still air. A head wind now would be worse than a calamity. It would be fatal, inevitably fatal. However, his fears proved groundless, and the aircraft reached its base with only failure to report.

'Refuel and take over,' Biggles told Algy wearily. 'Try a different track.' He started as if a thought had occurred to him. A puzzled frown creased his forehead. 'By the way, where's the whaler?'

Algy shrugged. 'She hasn't come.'

Biggles's frown deepened. 'Hasn't come? What the deuce can she be doing?'

'The bally storm may have delayed her,' suggested Bertie.

'Of course it would,' acknowledged Biggles. 'But a whaler is built for salt water and she'd see it through. Storm or no storm she should have been here before this. Good Lord!' His eyes opened wide. He pursed his lips. 'I wonder…'

'Wonder what?' prompted Algy.

'That ship is loaded with oil and von Schonbeck knows it. I wonder if he's had the nerve to turn back and… It's the sort of thing he might do. I ought to be kicked for not considering the possibility.'

'I wouldn't worry,' said Algy. 'There's probably a simple explanation for the delay. It's far more likely that the whaler slipped under the lee of Kerguelen while the storm was on instead of battering her way against it.'

'It might be,' agreed Biggles. 'I'll tell you what, Algy. Fill up with petrol, and for a start fly back towards Corbie Island to see if you can spot the whaler coming. That'll settle any argument. Take Bertie with you for a breath of fresh air. This hut stinks like the fo'c'sle of a Dutch onion boat.'

'Here, I say, old boy, I was only making Irish stew,' protested Bertie. 'Jolly good stew, too. Try some?'

'We'll take a chance,' agreed Biggles, smiling.

Algy went off, taking Bertie with him, and soon afterwards the roar of engines announced their departure.

As Algy swung round the northern tip of the island on a course for Corbie, he flew as a man flies on a simple routine operation. He was quite sure that he would see the whaler ploughing along bound for the aircraft base, and the last thing he expected was anything in the nature of excitement. And at first events fell out much as he expected. In five minutes he spotted the whaler slogging along the lee of Kerguelen, northward bound.

'There she is,' he told Bertie casually. 'I was right. She's been sheltering from the storm. I'll go down and give them a wave; then we'll beetle back and let Biggles know it's okay.'

In accordance with this simple programme Algy cut his engines and, altering course slightly, began a long glide towards the ship. But as he drew near his easy attitude changed. He stiffened, bending forward to peer through the windscreen. Bertie did the same.

'Am I seeing things or is there something queer about that ship?' muttered Algy.

Bertie screwed his monocle in his eye and looked again. 'If you ask me, old boy, I'd say she's been dragged through hell backwards. Must have been the bally storm that knocked her about – what?'

'Not on your life,' snapped Algy. 'The wave wasn't created yet that could tear that hole in her side. She's been shelled, and hit – and hit hard. By thunder! Biggles was right. Von Schonbeck has been at her again. I'm going down.'

'Here, take it easy, old boy,' murmured Bertie uncomfortably. 'She may have the beastly Nazis on board, and all that.'

'No!' shouted Algy, as they swept low over the whaler. 'That's Axel standing on the wheelhouse. He's waving. He wouldn't be allowed to do that if there were Nazis on board. I'm going to risk it.'

He swung round, dropped a wing and side-slipped down, to land and come to rest about a cable's length from the whaler. Axel appeared at the rail, beckoning, so he taxied on until by scrambling along a wing he was able to grab a rope which Axel threw to him. In a minute he was aboard. 'What's happened?' he asked breathlessly.

He asked the question automatically, for he knew what the answer would be. At any rate, he had a pretty good idea of it. The condition of the ship, as he saw it from close range, told its own story. On reaching the deck a swift glance around confirmed everything, if confirmation were needed. The superstructure was a wreck. Standing gear was a shell-torn tangle. Splinters lay everywhere. There were bloodstains. Old Leatherface sat at the foot of the mainmast, cheeks grey under their tan. Some members of the crew were trying to clear up the mess. Pumps were working. All this Algy took in at a glance before turning horrified questioning eyes at Axel.

'The submarine shelled us – but we still have the ship,' announced Axel, smiling ruefully.

'But what happened?' persisted Algy.

'When the storm was bad, being short-handed we decided to run into the cove at the southern end of the island for the night,' said Axel simply. 'The submarine was there. We did not know it. It was dark, very dark. But in the morning there she was, getting oil from the tank on shore. There was much oil on the water. It may be the oil from the tank, or perhaps what your captain said was right, and the submarine is damaged. I do not know. But when we are seen the Nazis run to their guns and fire. We slip our cable and back out, but we are hit many times. It was bad.'

'When was this?' asked Algy quickly.

'This morning.'

'And where is the submarine now?'

'When last I see her she is in the cove.'

Algy's manner became brittle. 'Can you handle the ship?'

'Yes. We are making water, but hands are at the pumps and I think we shall be well.'

'Good. Bring her along. I must let my chief know about this.'

'Yes.'

'See you later.'

Algy scrambled back along the wing to drop into the cockpit. 'The submarine has been at Kerguelen all along,' he told Bertie tersely. 'She's lying in the cove at the southern tip of the island, presumably the one where Biggles found the dump. The whaler tried to get in and was shelled. Axel says she was still there when he left. I'm getting back.'

The engines roared, and the aircraft, after cutting a creamy scar across the black water, rose into the air. Five minutes later it was down again, at its base. Algy jumped ashore and raced for the hut. As he neared it the door was thrown open and Biggles appeared, his facing asking a question, as if he had seen Algy's haste.

'What is it?' he demanded sharply.

In a few words Algy reported the position.

'Stiffen the crows!' exclaimed Biggles furiously. 'And I didn't guess it. No matter. We should get him now. He can't have got far.'

'He'll dive when he sees us,' warned Algy.

'If he's out of the cove he will.'

'What then?'

'I'll bring him up with depth-charges.'

'You'll be more likely to sink him – and he's got the gold aboard.'

'Okay, then I'll sink him,' rasped Biggles. 'But I'm not letting him get away. He may still be in the cove, taking in oil or repairing his ship. If he is, we've got him. We'll shut him in.'

'How?'

'By blasting the entrance of the cove. It's very narrow. Or better still, we'll bottle him in by using the whaler as a block ship. We'll sink her across the entrance.

'The owners won't be pleased if you sink their ship.'

'What's a whaler when five million pounds are at stake?' rapped out Biggles. 'I'll tell you what I'm going to do. Taking depth-charges I'm going to the cove, dropping you at the whaler on the way. Tell Axel to turn his ship round, and under all the steam he can raise make back for the cove. He's to get her crossways across the entrance and open his seacocks. If the sub tries to get out he must ram her. We shall already be there, holding her in. If von Schonbeck tries to get out I'll lay a couple of depth-charges across his bows. The great thing now is speed.'

'What do I do when the ship sinks under me?' asked Algy coldly.

'Swim,' answered Biggles shortly. 'But if you have any sense you'll have a boat ready to take the ship's company ashore. You should be able to hold the Nazis if they come for you. We'll do our best to help you. But the first thing is to get the sub bottled up. It's no use planning beyond that. Afterwards we'll see how things go.'

'And if the sub is already at sea?'

'I'll plaster her. If you see that happen tell Axel to bring the whaler here.'

'Okay,' agreed Algy.

'Let's get cracking,' said Biggles.

CHAPTER XIV

The Pace Quickens

With full tanks, two depth-charges, and the entire party on board, Biggles took off and raced low towards the last known position of the whaler. It was still there, so he landed, and after a few words with Axel, outlining the plan and telling him what he wanted him to do, he took off again and headed for the submarine's hiding-place, leaving Algy on board. Fifteen minutes later it came into view, with oil spreading out in a broad fan-shaped stain from the narrow entrance, and from then on the action was swift and fierce.

It was at once evident that the aircraft had arrived just in time – in time, that is, to prevent the U-boat from gaining the open sea, where no doubt it would have submerged and perhaps disappeared for all time. The submarine, with von Schonbeck and several members of the crew on deck, was moving towards the channel at a speed which suggested that he had heard the aircraft coming and was now trying to extricate himself from a position that might well prove desperate. He had in fact almost reached the channel by the time the aircraft was over the scene.

The reception the *Tarpon* received was much as Biggles expected. No amount of camouflage could help the

U-boat now. It could only fight. The crew jumped to their action stations and flak came streaming up. Biggles was ready for it. He promptly took evading action, and diving low dropped his first depth-charge in the channel, partly in the hope of blocking it by a landslide or to cause the U-boat to swerve. Not knowing the depth of the water in the cove, which might turn out to be too deep for salvage operations, he did not attempt to get a direct hit, which he might well have scored. In one respect he was successful. A great spout of water leapt high into the air. As it subsided it piled itself into a mighty wave which struck the U-boat a glancing blow across the bows before half burying her under foam which swept across her deck and carried overboard at least two members of a gun crew.

The effect of this was to throw the U-boat off its course so that for a little while it was in some risk of colliding head-on with the cliff. To save his ship von Schonbeck was forced to continue the turning movement. He made a half-circle, narrowly missing some rocks, so that by the time the manoeuvre was complete the U-boat was stern first to the entrance – a state of affairs which suited Biggles very well, for a start, anyway. All this time flak was coming up, and it continued to come up, so that conditions in the aircraft were far from comfortable. Indeed, as far as Ginger was concerned it looked like being the final showdown. Either the aircraft or the submarine, in service slang, was about to 'have it'. But as it turned out the end was not yet, although it was getting close.

Biggles, feeling that he now had the whip-hand, sheered off a little to see what von Schonbeck would do. He was too old a hand to take more chances than were demanded. The Nazi did not keep him waiting. With its propellers creaming the water the U-boat turned again towards the entrance, as if determined at all costs to escape from the trap in which it now found itself. Biggles was equally determined that it should not get out. He waited a little while, turning constantly to spoil the aim of the gunners, and then went down in another steep dive. Von Schonbeck must have known what he intended, but there was nothing he could do about it. He had no room to manoeuvre, for any sort of turn would involve him in a collision with the cliffs guarding the entrance.

Biggles let go his second depth-charge, and this time it looked as if it would hit the U-boat. It nearly did. It burst so close that it half lifted the submarine out of the water, and at the same time threw her on her beam ends with such violence that before she could recover her steel hull had scraped against a projecting shoulder of rock with sufficient force to make her reel again. It was obvious to those in the air that she must have been damaged, and the action her commander took practically confirmed it. The U-boat began to travel hard astern towards the landing beach by the depot.

This Biggles only saw in a fleeting glance, for his attention was now fully occupied with the plane. A shell, one of the last to be fired, had burst under the tail unit, inflicting such damage as to cause it to become almost unmanageable. Indeed, for a minute or two those on board thought they were quite out of control. Biggles managed to make some sort of recovery, but realising that it was not possible to remain airborne without risk of a serious crash he looked about for a place to get down. He might, of course, have landed on the water, but he felt it was almost certain that his keel had been damaged by shell splinters. Moreover, it would mean landing in the cove, in which case he would become a sitting target for the submarine's guns. That, obviously, was out of the question. The only flat area round the actual cove was the beach for which the U-boat was making. That, for equally obvious reasons, was no use. As far as the rest of the island within gliding distance was concerned there was only one reasonable area. This was what appeared to be a slightly undulating expanse of moss that topped the cliff near the entrance and fell back towards the main terrain of the island. It was on this that Biggles decided to put the aircraft down, so lowering his wheels he put the plan into execution. The aircraft bumped, bounced, bounced again, and then, dragging in the moss and squelching water under its wheels, it ran on to a groggy landing, to finish one wing down due to the wheel on that side sinking deep into the moss. A stream of machine-gun bullets whistling past the tip of the exposed wing made it abundantly clear that the airmen were not yet out of danger, although fortunately a long, low fold in the ground near the rim of the cliff protected the lower part of the aircraft, including most of the hull.

'Outside everybody,' snapped Biggles. 'Keep your heads down.'

Those in the machine jumped clear and dived for cover. A few more bullets came whizzing over, then an uneasy silence fell. With brackish peat water oozing through the moss under his weight Biggles crawled to the top of the rising ground, and peeping over saw the U-boat, apparently beached, near the depot. Not a soul was in sight, so after watching for a little while he dropped back to the others.

'We've given von Schonbeck something to think about, anyway,' he announced, with satisfaction in his voice. 'All the same, we're not sitting very pretty ourselves. In fact, we seem to have arrived at a state of stalemate. The sub is damaged, no doubt of that, but how badly we don't know. Unfortunately we're on the carpet ourselves so there's nothing more we can do. What I mean is, if von Schonbeck decides that his damage isn't serious, and tries to rush the entrance, we've no means of stopping him. Our big chance is, right now, to block the entrance with the whaler and seal the submarine in before von Schonbeck can get moving again. The whaler isn't due yet, but she must be getting close. The next two hours ought to settle things one way or another.'

'In the meantime, old boy, what do we do?' demanded Bertie.

'First of all we'll have a look at the machine to see how bad the damage is,' answered Biggles. 'If we can't get her off again we're going to have an awful long walk home. If you like, Bertie, you can take a rifle and try sniping anybody you see moving about the sub, but they're either inside or else they've taken cover in one of tire huts. Keep watch, but don't get sniped yourself.'

'Not me – no bally fear,' declared Bertie, going off to fetch the rifle.

Biggles and Ginger examined the machine. The damage was serious but not vital. Elevator controls had been cut and there were some nasty holes through the tailplanes, fin and rudder, but there was nothing that could not be repaired, temporarily, given time. Biggles decided to start work right away.

From time to time Bertie, from his selected position, passed back information. 'I think the blighters are inside their beastly sardine can,' he called. 'I can hear 'em banging about. Straightening things out, and so on. There's a lot of oil round her.'

'I should say von Schonbeck is doing some quick patching up with a view to getting out before we hit him again,' said Biggles. 'He must have seen us go down. He may think he has plenty of time. Our trump card, the whaler, will shake him when it turns up and sinks itself in the entrance of his bolthole. Keep an eye open for the ship, Bertie, and let me know when she turns up.'

Biggles and Ginger carried on with their work. Time wore on without any new development. A feeble sun, blinking mistily through the clouds, climbed over its zenith and began to sink towards the west.

'The tide's coming in. I believe it's floated the sub off the beach,' called Bertie.

A quarter of an hour later he spoke again. 'She's started her engines. She's moving.'

Biggles frowned. 'I shall be sick if she manages to slip out after all,' he muttered to Ginger.

'Is there nothing we can do to stop her?'

'Not a thing,' returned Biggles. 'If the whaler doesn't turn up we're helpless – anyway, until we can get back to base for more depth-charges.'

'Here they come!' shouted Bertie. His rifle cracked, and cracked again.

The bang of a gun and the scream of a shell made Ginger jump.

'What goes on?' called Biggles.

'It's the whaler!' yelled Bertie. 'She's nosing into the entrance – didn't see her before – bally cliff was in the way. Jolly good show.'

Biggles and Ginger dropped what they were doing and, crouching low, ran to the top of the rise. Biggles took one look and snapped, 'Get another rifle, Ginger.'

A three-sided battle, if battle it can be called, now developed. The U-boat directed its fire against the whaler, whose purpose by this time must have been apparent. A machine-gunner, from behind a steel shield, directed his fire along the top of the cliff to protect the submarine's gun crews at whom Biggles and Bertie were sniping. This state of affairs, however, did not last long, one reason being that the whaler was now in the channel, and it was evident that should a collision occur between the whaler and the U-boat, the latter would get the worst of the deal. The submarine stopped, and then began to back towards the beach she had just left. Its guns continued firing and the whaler came in for a good deal of punishment.

'They've done their stuff,' said Biggles suddenly. 'Axel has opened his seacocks. The whaler's settling down. Von Schonbeck must realise it. He knows it's all up. At least, he knows he'll never get out of that cove without a lot of high explosive to shift our block-ship. I can see Algy. They're lowering a boat – about time, too. Not seeing the machine Algy will wonder what has happened to us. We'd better let him know where we are so that he can join us.' Dropping back and crouching low to keep out of sight of those on the U-boat, Biggles ran along the top of the cliff to a point immediately above the whaler. Then, by shouting, he made contact.

It was half an hour before the crew of the whaler joined those on the cliff, for as they were unable to scale the cliff with two wounded men the boat had to be taken to a beach outside the entrance and a landing effected there. However, at the end, the two parties were united on the cliff near the aircraft.

Algy arrived smiling. 'We've put the cork in the bottle,' he announced. 'Von Schonbeck is inside for keeps.'

'He's inside for some time, anyway,' agreed Biggles. 'But I wouldn't bet too much on keeping him there indefinitely. He's a cunning devil.' Briefly he explained how the aircraft came to be grounded.

'What's the next move, then?' asked Algy.

'I haven't decided yet,' answered Biggles. He glanced at the sky. 'It's getting dark. We look like being here for the night. Von Schonbeck may not be content to leave us here though, covering the submarine, and the entrance to the channel, as we do, so we'd better get into some sort of position for defence.' Biggles broke off and thought for a moment. 'I think the time has come to let Raymond know how things stand,' he continued. 'With the U-boat immobilised von Schonbeck could do nothing even if he picked up the signal. Yes, I think that's the best thing. I shall have to remain here to see what happens. The machine should fly all right now, although it wouldn't do to chuck it about. I'll tell you what, Algy. Take Bertie and the wounded Norwegians with you and push along to the base. Make radio contact with Raymond. Tell him the story and how we're fixed. Ask him for instructions, or alternatively, ask him to do something about it. Daylight should last just about long enough to see you home. In the morning you'd better come back here to let me know what Raymond says. Meanwhile, the rest of us will stay here and keep an eye on things. Von Schonbeck may try something. A Nazi of his type isn't finished until he's dead.'

'Okay,' agreed Algy. 'You're sure the machine's all right?'

'She'll fly, and your engines are okay, but you may find her a bit groggy on rudder control.'

Algy nodded, and moved quickly to carry out his instructions, for the light was fast fading. The wounded Norwegians were lifted into the machine. Bertie followed.

'Don't let that blighter do us out of the gold,' he adjured Biggles. 'I've always wanted a nice big piece of gold to play with.'

'I'll watch it,' promised Biggles smiling.

With no small anxiety those who were to stay watched the machine take off and disappear into the northern sky. No flak came up. In the vicinity of the submarine all remained quiet. The only sounds were the murmur of the eternal waves fretting along the shore, and the plaintive cries of the gulls.

'Tomorrow, I think, should see the showdown,' opined Biggles.

CHAPTER XV

The Clock that Ticked Again

Dawn broke dull and drear, with a suspicion of frost and a threat of snow in the air. It found the little party on the cliff chattering with cold, and, with the exception of Biggles, who appeared oblivious to weather conditions, with small enthusiasm for the work ahead. Even Axel, who was on watch, glowered into the thin grey mist that enveloped them, reducing visibility to a hundred yards so that the submarine could not be seen, although its position could, with fair accuracy, be judged. No sound came from the U-boat. In fact, it was a long time since any sound had been heard, apart from the lap of water against rock.

Ginger spoke. His face was pale and nipped from the penetrating cold. 'I wish this infernal mist would lift,' he muttered. 'Algy will never risk flying in this stuff.'

'The trouble is, at this time of the year it may go on for days,' answered Biggles. 'We've got to be prepared for that. On the other hand it may blow away. It only needs a slant of wind to shift it, and wind is a common commodity in these parts.'

'What the dickens are we going to do?' asked Ginger. 'If we going on sitting here I'm liable to die of starvation – if I don't freeze to death first.'

'I've no intention of staying here,' returned Biggles. 'That silence across the cove isn't natural. Von Schonbeck should be doing something. Dash it, he *must* be doing something. But what? I'm going to find out.'

Ginger's eyebrows went up. 'You mean, you're going to have a crack at him?'

'Not necessarily,' answered Biggles. 'But if this fog doesn't clear in an hour I'm going to make a reconnaissance of the beach to find out what is going on there.'

'Alone?'

Biggles considered the question. 'No,' he decided. 'In this sort of weather I'm all against breaking up my force while it can be kept intact. There are nine of us all told, and with pistols and rifles we're pretty well armed. Just how many men von Schonbeck has available we don't know, but he hasn't as many as he had. We've whittled them down a bit. Assuming that he started with twenty he can't have more than ten or a dozen left. Of course, they're better equipped than we are because they've got machine-guns, but even so I think we ought to be able to put up a fair show if it comes to a scrap.'

After that they fell silent again. It grew a little lighter, but the mist still clung like a clammy veil to the knoll on which the party squatted. Biggles looked at his watch and got up.

'Okay,' he said. 'I'm not waiting any longer. Let's move along and see what goes on. We'll form up in line, keeping in sight of each other, and move slowly down the hill to approach the beach from the rear. If there's trouble we can retreat back here. I don't think von Schonbeck will risk trying to dislodge us because he would be bound to have casualties, and if he loses any more of his crew he won't have enough to man his ship. All right, let's move along. No talking. We shall be able to move quietly over this moss. With luck we ought to be able to get pretty close to the submarine without being seen. If we can pick off a few of them so well and good, but I don't want any firing until I give the word. Is that clear, Axel?'

Axel answered that he understood perfectly, and repeated the orders in his own language to those of his countrymen who knew no English. The party, keeping in line and with weapons at the ready, then moved off, descending a long incline which ended at the same level as the beach and perhaps a quarter of a mile from it, with a fold of rising ground between the two areas. Ginger moved next in line to Biggles. The uncanny silence persisted. With deep moss underfoot the advancing party might have been a line of slate-coloured ghosts.

The first objective, the dip at the foot of the incline, was reached without incident. Still no sound came from the submarine, and to Ginger the eerie silence took on the unreal character of a dream. In the dip Biggles halted the line by a signal, and by a sweep of his arm swung it round directly towards the beach. The march was resumed. Still no sound came from the submarine.

The near end of the beach came into view and the advance became more cautious. At the point where the moss gave way to shingle Biggles halted and peered ahead, eyes trying to probe the mist. He could just vaguely make out the shape of the U-boat, but it was still indistinct and there was no movement of any sort. He went on again, his body tense, pistol gripped in his right hand, halting for a moment after each step. Still nothing happened. Gradually things began to take shape – the hull of the submarine with the conning tower rising from it, a line of debris along the high-water mark and the squat stone houses beyond.

Biggles beckoned Ginger nearer. 'Pass word along the line to beware of booby traps,' he said softly. 'There may be an ambush. If firing starts remember that we retire on the knoll.'

Ginger nodded and went off on his errand, leaving Biggles staring at the submarine.

By single paces Biggles advanced again, eyes switching from one object to another, nerves braced from the strain of expecting every step to end the uncanny silence.

Still nothing happened. A black-headed gull swung on rigid pinions over the steel hull and with a mournful cry soared into the mist whence it had appeared. Biggles went on until he stood near the water's edge less than twenty paces from the U-boat. Dirty, oil- and weather-stained, it had the appearance of an abandoned hulk. The conning tower was open. He stood there motionless, surveying the scene, for perhaps five minutes. Then he signalled to the party to rally on him. One by one they came, in silence.

'If this is a trap it ought to have been sprung by now,' Biggles said to Ginger, who was the first to arrive. 'I don't get it. There's something unnatural about this set-up. What the devil is von Schonbeck doing? He can't have just shut himself up in his ship.'

'Maybe they're in one of the huts,' suggested Ginger.

'Even so, you'd think they'd put out a guard, and a guard would have seen us by now – unless he's asleep. I can't imagine anyone under von Schonbeck's command going to sleep on duty. However, we'll soon settle it. Stand fast while I have a look round.'

Standing on the beach Ginger watched Biggles advance warily to the nearest hut, look inside, and pass on to the next. It seemed to be asking for trouble. Every second he expected to hear a shot and see Biggles fall, and cold as he was, perspiration broke out on his forehead from the strain of waiting. He drew a deep breath when Biggles came back and joined the party.

'They've pulled out,' he said shortly. 'It's the only possible answer. That's something I did *not* expect, unless...' Biggles walked on a little way and then, stopping suddenly, pointed to a line of torn and buckled plates in the submarine's side. 'That must be the answer,' he said. 'That must have happened when she collided with the rock. Von Schonbeck daren't take his ship to sea in that state, and I doubt, even if he had unlimited time at his disposal, whether he could make good the damage. Yes, that's it. Bottled in by the whaler and with his ship out of action he must have decided that nothing was to be gained by staying here. He's taken to the country. Watch your step. Don't forget what happened the last time we were on this beach.'

'What are we going to do?' queried Ginger.

'We might as well have a look inside the ship as we're so close,' answered Biggles.

'But von Schonbeck wouldn't leave the gold behind,' asserted Ginger.

'No. If they've gone I imagine they'll have taken it with them, or buried it somewhere,' returned Biggles. 'But we'll have a look round inside all the same.'

Motioning the others to wait, Biggles waded out to the U-boat, climbed on board the deck and made his way to the conning tower, taking Ginger with him. At a distance of half a dozen paces he halted and called sharply. 'Von Schonbeck!'

There was no answer.

Biggles called again. 'I'm waiting for you,' he added.

Still no answer.

Biggles shrugged. 'I don't think he's here,' he said in a low voice. 'We'll soon make sure.' He went on to the conning tower, mounted it and looked down. For perhaps half a minute he waited. Then he climbed in and disappeared from sight.

Ginger hurried after him, and looking down saw Biggles standing pistol in hand at the foot of the steps near the periscope control. He went down and, joining his chief, looked about him in curiosity, conscious of a queer sensation now that he was actually standing in the ship they had come so far to find. All around were the intricate instruments and equipment of the U-boat. He noticed a conspicuous clock. It had stopped at one minute to twelve. An unnatural hush possessed the ship, unnatural because with so much mechanism about he felt that some of it should be working. But nothing moved. The silence was the dead utter silence of the tomb.

It was perhaps on this account that a sound, when it came, was all the more noticeable. Without speaking Biggles moved forward a few paces, quietly, to get a clearer view of the gangway leading aft. It was as he did this that the sound came. The clock had begun to tick. Biggles eyes flashed to it, so did Ginger's. Biggles looked at the steel floor on which they stood. Ginger's eyes followed, wonderingly, surprised and not a little alarmed at the sudden stiffening in Biggles's attitude. He saw, lying across the floor, a thin strand of copper wire, a strand so fine that had it not been for the light catching its untarnished surface it would not have been noticeable. It was broken, and lay curled back on itself like a spring.

Biggles spoke. He said one word. He uttered it in a voice so clipped that Ginger obeyed it on the instant. The word was: 'Bolt!'

Even as Ginger shot up the conning tower steps he had a shrewd idea of what was happening, or what was about to happen. Reaching the deck he did not stop, but ran along to the nearest point of the beach, jumped ashore, and went on running. He could hear Biggles close behind him. 'Bolt!' he shouted to Axel, who, with his rifle half raised, was looking at him in astonishment.

'Run for your lives!' shouted Biggles, as he took a flying leap on to the shingle.

The entire party raced along the beach.

It had covered about a hundred yards when from behind there came such an explosion as Ginger had never heard. An instant later what felt like a solid wall of air struck him in the back and threw him forward on his face. Half dazed by the shock he started to pick himself up, aware that there were others in positions similar to himself. A movement behind made him turn still further. He was just in time to see the submarine settling back into the water. The centre part was still raised high, but it had broken across the middle. Above it towered a mighty column of smoke. From the beach near the entrance of the cove sped a terrifying tidal wave. It struck the cliffs that guarded the entrance flinging spray nearly to the top, and then rebounded.

'Look out!' shouted Biggles, and scrambling to his feet he made for the rising ground behind the camp.

The wave, with the relentless force of an express train, came after them. It all but had them. The curling crest crashed forward and down some thirty yards behind them so that the spreading rush of water licked their heels. Then it was all over. The wave receded. The water in the cove boiled for a little while, then fell quiet. Hard against the beach lay the U-boat, its hull distorted, its back broken.

Biggles sat and looked at it for a minute without speaking. Then he laughed quietly. 'What a beauty,' he murmured.

'What's a beauty?' demanded Ginger.

'That booby trap,' answered Biggles. 'I never saw a better one.'

'We nearly didn't see that one,' growled Ginger.

'You're right. It was pretty close,' admitted Biggles. 'Had we been talking we shouldn't have heard the clock start ticking, and had the clock not started ticking I shouldn't have spotted that wire.' He smiled. 'If we hadn't spotted the wire we should have made the fastest take-off ever. I should think the bomb, or whatever it was, exploded in the U-boat's remaining store of torpedoes and shells. Von Schonbeck must have heard the bang. From where he is he can probably see the smoke. Only an intruder in the submarine could have set off the bomb, so by this time he is no doubt having a chuckle at our expense and patting himself on the back for his ingenuity. He's justified, mind you. He might have got the lot of us at one go. He's going to have a horrid disappointment though when we turn up again.'

'Algy and Bertie must have heard that bang, too,' remarked Ginger. 'They'll be worried.'

Biggles glanced at the sky. 'The murk's lifting,' he observed. 'A clear sky will bring Algy along hotfoot to see what goes on. Hark!'

Faintly on the still air came the drone of an aircraft.

Ginger cocked an ear and listened. 'Okay – that's the *Tarpon*,' he announced. 'Algy has only to make a dud landing now and we *are* in the soup.'

'Let's go back to the cliff and show ourselves,' suggested Biggles.

CHAPTER XVI

Biggles Offers Terms

The party hastened back to the top of the hill. By the time they had reached it the mist had been lifted by a watery sun and the aircraft was circling preparatory to coming in. To Ginger's unspeakable relief it made a safe landing, whereupon the party moved forward to meet Algy and Bertie who now descended.

Algy's first words were, 'What the deuce was that bang?'

Biggles told him, jerking a thumb in the direction of the shattered U-boat. 'Did you make contact with Raymond? That's the important thing at the moment,' he asked.

'Yes, we got through without any trouble,' returned Algy. 'It took some time but I gave him the complete gen.'

'What did he say to that?' inquired Biggles.

'He said okay, stand by.'

Biggles frowned. 'Stand by for what?'

Algy shrugged. 'He didn't say.'

'Well, I call that pretty good. How long does he expect us to stand here?'

'I imagine he'd have to do some thinking before he made a plan of operation.'

Biggles nodded. 'Maybe he thought it unwise to announce his plans over the air in case the wrong people picked up the signal. All the same, I wish I knew what he intended doing. Von Schonbeck is on the move, he's got the bullion with him so it won't do to leave him too long to his own devices.'

'But he can't get off the island, old boy – if you see what I mean?' put in Bertie.

'I'm not so sure of that,' answered Biggles, looking round. 'That fellow will be a menace until he's dead and buried.'

'But even if he got away he couldn't take the gold with him,' said Algy.

With his hands thrust deep in his pockets and his head bent, Biggles paced up and down. 'Let's try to get the thing in line,' he said curtly. 'Von Schonbeck knew that he was in a trap – there was no escape out of the cove, anyway. The only course for him, when you come to think about it, was to retire to the interior of the island taking the gold with him. What next? Well, five millions in gold is something. A man with five million pounds' worth of metal is in a position to bargain.'

'For what, old lad? I don't get it,' murmured Bertie, polishing his eyeglass.

'His life, for one thing. Suppose he buries that gold. Who is going to find it on an island this size? That you can't dig up an entire island is proved by the fact that there is still a twelve-million-pound treasure on Cocos Island, although scores of people have tried to find it – and Cocos is nothing like the size of Kerguelen. Very well. Let us say we go after von Schonbeck and catch him. Or suppose the Government landed troops here and rounded him up. He just smiles blandly and says okay. Hang me if you like, but if you do bang goes your gold. He may say, let me go and I'll tell you where the gold is. So what? The gold doesn't mean much to us. For one thing it isn't ours, anyway. But the people who actually own the gold might be willing to bargain. What is one man's life to a fortune? But it may not come to that. The point is, von Schonbeck, by pulling out, is still at large with the gold. He's gaining time if nothing else. If he could get away, get clear of the island, he might return later for the gold.'

'How could he get away?' asked Algy. 'If we leave him here he's likely to be marooned for the rest of his life.'

'Don't you believe it,' said Biggles scornfully. 'To start with I've got an idea that he's got a boat with him. They were using a collapsible boat to repair the damage round the stern of the U-boat at Corbie Island. That boat was housed just aft of the conning tower – but it wasn't on the sub when we boarded her just now. Von Schonbeck may have that boat with him. The scoundrel is a seaman – we must grant him that. With decent weather he might push off and make a landfall at some other island. Long trips have more than once been made in an open boat. Of course, he wouldn't be so crazy as to attempt to take the gold, but if he got away he'd find it easy enough to come back later on, in a ship of some size, and collect the bullion. Amongst the German settlements in South America he'd find plenty of ships' captains willing to take a chance on that.'

'This is all supposing that he has a small boat,' put in Axel, who had followed Biggles's argument with profound interest.

'All right, let's suppose he hasn't a boat,' replied Biggles. 'That doesn't mean we can just stand by waiting for Raymond to do something. If once von Schonbeck gets into the mountains of the interior it would need an army to get him out. To bring here the number of men that would be required for the search, together with stores and equipment, would cost nearly as much in cash as the gold is worth. What would be the alternative? To leave him here, marooned? To leave that bunch of Nazis on the loose would be like leaving a pack of wolves. Don't forget that once in a while ships call here – whalers, sealers, and so on. Von Schonbeck and his bunch would grab the first one to come in, scupper the crew and get away with it. One factor which we must never forget is this, von Schonbeck knows that his neck is practically in a noose if he is caught, and desperate men take chances.'

'So what's the answer?' asked Ginger helplessly.

'There can be only one,' returned Biggles. 'We've got to go after von Schonbeck. We've got to locate him, watch him, and if possible keep him on the move, so that he gets no chance to bury the gold. I needn't point out the snag in that. We've got to find him and catch up with him before darkness falls. Give von Schonbeck one night in these hills and if I know the man he'll appear to-morrow without the gold. He can't have got a great way yet. Hearing the explosion he may take his time, supposing that we've been blown sky-high as he intended, and as we jolly nearly were.'

'And having spotted him what do we do about it?' asked Ginger, a trifle sarcastically. 'Our rifles and pistols will make a poor showing against the machine-guns which we know they've got – at least, I imagine they won't have left them behind.'

'I'll grant you that,' agreed Biggles. 'All I can say is, we'll deal with that situation when the time comes. Man for man we must be pretty evenly matched.'

'The first thing is to find the blighters – find 'em, that's the thing,' declared Bertie.

'Bertie,' said Biggles evenly, 'you've said it. Let's get mobile.'

'We can't all get in the plane,' Axel pointed out.

'There's no need – yet. I'll take my three friends with me. You'll stay here with your party, Axel, and keep guard over the remains of the submarine. Should by any remote chance reinforcements arrive from my chief, Air Commodore Raymond, you can tell them where we are and what we are doing.'

Leaving the Norwegians on the cliff the others climbed into the aircraft. Biggles took off and headed for the interior of the island.

'See what I mean about looking for a few men in that mess,' he remarked to Ginger, indicating the gaunt rugged mountains which piled up behind rolling foothills that came down nearly to the sea. 'Finding a needle in a haystack would be easy compared with digging out a handful of men from that mass of rock. But von Schonbeck can't have reached the mountains yet.'

'This is not going to be a very nice place for a forced landing,' murmured Ginger, regarding the terrain below and in front of them with misgivings, and remembering the patched-up condition of their aircraft.

Biggles smiled faintly. 'We've flown over worse country.'

'Maybe, but I don't think you ever heard me say that I enjoyed it,' replied Ginger.

The unexplored interior of the island now presented a panorama as forbidding as could be imagined. Near at hand, the first impression was of a bleak, lonely expanse of rolling moorland, dotted everywhere with dark grey stone, either loose boulders or outcrops of the bedrock. The low areas were occupied by sheets of black, evil-looking water of unknown depth. Beyond this foreground, as the terrain rose it broke into tier after tier of rock ridges terminating in a tremendous massif of peaks, with glaciers streaking the ravines and depressions. What lay in the valleys between the mountain ranges was a matter for conjecture, for all that could be seen from the air was sombre shadows through which water, spilling off the rock slopes in numerous falls and cascades, forced a tortuous course. In one place smoke rose in a tenuous cloud, betraying the volcanic nature of the island. Looking at this harsh picture Ginger found it easy to understand why the island had never been properly explored, much less surveyed.

Biggles pointed to a pass that cut through the nearest range; it looked as though it had been smashed open by a giant axe. 'If von Schonbeck wants to get into the mountains that's the way he'll go,' he asserted. 'There's no other way that I can see. We'll try that one first, anyway.'

The *Tarpon*, flying at a thousand feet, roared on, and five minutes later Biggles's surmise matured into fact. 'There they are,' he said briefly.

Peering down the others saw a line of men, mostly in pairs, moving like sluggish ants towards the pass. They were as yet perhaps two miles from it, having covered some ten to twelve miles since leaving the sea.

'The dirty dogs haven't made a lot of ground,' observed Bertie.

'That ground is probably a lot rougher than it looks,' answered Biggles. 'Moreover, they wouldn't be able to take a straight line. They'd have to go round the lakes, and those outcrops of rock. Apart from that, look at the loads they're carrying.'

'The bullion boxes,' breathed Ginger.

'That's why they're marching in pairs,' said Biggles. 'For two men one of those boxes must be a heavy load, but von Schonbeck isn't going to leave it behind – no fear. There he is, marching ahead. He's looking up at us – you can see his face.'

'They haven't got the boat with them,' observed Algy.

'They may have parked it somewhere near the sea. As it is, they're carrying about as much as they can manage.'

Ginger could see the men. 'Fourteen,' he counted aloud. 'One way and another we seem to have accounted for a few since we started.'

'How about accounting for a few more?' suggested Algy. 'Our fixed guns need warming up – we haven't used them yet.'

Biggles did not answer immediately. He went into a wide flat turn, watching the men below struggling on, obviously with difficulty, towards the hills.

'We can't go on flying round them indefinitely. Next thing we shall be out of petrol,' prompted Ginger.

'I'm going to give them a chance,' decided Biggles.

'Nobody in his right mind gives a mad tiger a chance,' growled Ginger. 'Nazis don't appreciate chances; they've proved that often enough. A chance will only give von Schonbeck an opportunity to trick you.'

'I don't think he'll do that,' returned Biggles softly. 'I can't help feeling that some of those men may be ready to pack up. They must know the game is finished. I hate killing a rat in a trap. A beast can't help being what it is. Pass me that message bag – or, better still, take over for a minute. Don't go too close to them.'

Ginger glanced at Algy, smiling wanly. Bertie's eyes met theirs in turn. Each know he was thinking the same thing. This was Biggles all over. Having got his man on the spot he had to give him a chance. That was his code, just as von Schonbeck's code was the Nazi code. It seemed silly – yet was it, wondered Ginger. A lot of people around the world respected this strange British idiosyncrasy.

They watched Biggles write his message and sign it. He read it over to them, 'Pack up. Leave the gold where it is. Start marching back and you will be treated as prisoners of war. Suggest you let your men decide for themselves. Continuance towards the mountains will signify your refusal of these terms, in which case we shall take action to stop you.'

Flying on over the fugitives he dropped it overboard. It fluttered down. Watching, those in the *Tarpon* saw it strike the ground about a hundred yards from the men, who halted while one of them ran out, picked it up and handed it to von Schonbeck. Dropping their loads the Germans mustered round their leader in a little group, a position in which they remained for some minutes, during which time the aircraft continued to circle.

'What goes on?' muttered Ginger suspiciously.

'They're probably talking it over,' returned Biggles, banking slightly to keep a clear view below. 'Hello!'

The ejaculation was prompted by a sudden movement. The group broke up in a manner which could only mean disagreement. Five men broke away from the main body and started running. Guns flashed. Puffs of smoke spurted. Three of the runners fell. One turned and fired back at the main body, scoring a hit. The two surviving runners went on to take cover behind an outcrop of rock.

'Some of them have had enough, anyway, and I don't wonder at that, when they see what's ahead of them,' murmured Biggles. 'Amazing, isn't it, how these Nazis so often finish up by shooting each other. God save us from such a hellish creed. Well, it looks as if von Schonbeck has decided to go on. He has lost six more of his men. That leaves eight. Yes, there they go. They're having to abandon some of the gold, but they're hanging on to as much as they can carry. Gold. Gold and blood. The old, old story. Funny how the two things go together. Well, if that's how von Schonbeck wants it, that's how he can have it. Hold your hats – we may get something back.' Biggles swung the *Tarpon* round and put its nose down in a steep dive.

A line of tracer bullets rose gracefully to meet it. Short jabbing flames spurted from the muzzles of the *Tarpon's* twin guns. Two lines of bullets flashed down.

CHAPTER XVII

Clean-up on Kerguelen

The result of the *Tarpon's* dive was to send the U-boat crew running for cover, of which plenty was available in the form of loose rock. Two men fell, although one of them, apparently only with a slight wound, continued to crawl on to what he evidently considered a safe place.

'That leaves six,' muttered Biggles, as he zoomed up after the attack. On the ground, all that could now be seen were the gold boxes, lying where they had been abandoned.

'Now what?' inquired Algy. 'You can't get 'em while they stay as they are. They can afford to stay there, but we can't hang around. As soon as it's dark they'll push along into the hills.'

'Every word you say is true,' agreed Biggles. 'That's why we can't allow that to happen. I'm going down.'

Ginger looked started. 'You mean – land?'

'There's nothing else we can do,' averred Biggles. 'It will start to get dark in an hour or two. We shan't have time to go home for more petrol. We'll settle this business right here and now. I'm not going to risk losing touch with von Schonbeck at this stage of the proceedings.'

'It'll be four of us against six, old boy,' Bertie pointed out.

'Oh no it won't,' returned Biggles evenly. 'As soon as we're on the carpet Algy can take off again and fetch Axel and his Norwegians. I'm sure they'll be glad to be in at the death.'

'By Jove! I say, that's an idea,' declared Bertie.

'Thank you,' acknowledged Biggles. 'The point is, where do we get down? I'd like it to be ahead of them if possible, or at any rate on their flank, so that we can keep them where they are. I hate walking, and if it comes to a race up those slopes we may lose.'

Casting about, Biggles descended on an area of what appeared to be smooth moss, between a quarter and a half a mile from the fugitives. Here, curiously enough – or it struck Ginger as curious at the time – there were no rocks, just a broad flat patch of thick sphagnum moss of many hues – green, yellow, orange, red. It was on this, after a cautious survey of the surface for obstructions, that Biggles landed. And as his wheels touched, and the full weight of the aircraft settled down on them, he knew that something was wrong. The machine rocked in a most extraordinary way, as if it were rolling on soft eccentric wheels. The others noticed it and looked through the side windows to see what caused the phenomenon.

Ginger cried, 'What the dickens!'

Then, suddenly, he knew. The aircraft *was* rocking, bouncing up and down with a slow sickening movement. All around, in the proximity of the aircraft, the earth seemed to be rocking, too. At first he thought that their landing had been coincidental with an earthquake – a not unnatural assumption, for that was the general impression created, and the island was, after all, volcanic. The moss was literally quaking – but not the distant view. The hills

174

were steady enough. The quake was curiously local. It was when he realised this that the first suspicion of the truth struck him, and when the truth did dawn on him his mouth went so dry with shock that he could hardly swallow.

The aircraft, still bouncing slightly, finished its forward run.

'Sit still everybody,' said Biggles, in a quiet but tense voice. 'We're on a bog.'

No one moved. No one spoke while the aircraft came gently to rest. The rocking movement ceased. The moss assumed its original firm appearance.

'Take it easy,' cautioned Biggles. 'Things may not be as bad as they seem.'

'I should jolly well hope not,' muttered Bertie, who had turned slightly pale. 'I once saw a chappie in a bog. He—'

'Tell us about it some other time,' interrupted Algy, through his teeth.

'Shut up a minute,' put in Biggles curtly. 'This is no time for fooling. You'd better get the hang of what's happened. We're on the worst sort of bog. What we have landed on is really a thick layer of scum, over water or soft mud, on which moss has grown. The scum is only floating. That's why it rocked when we touched down. The scum sagged under our weight. If our wheels break through the crust we can say good-bye to the aircraft. I should say the risk of that is pretty big at the moment because our weight is all concentrated on one spot. We must alter that. The only way we can do it is by getting out. Algy will stay. As soon as the others are out he'll take off – or try to.'

175

'What's wrong with taking off right away?' asked Ginger anxiously.

'I daren't risk trying to get off with this load on board. The lighter the machine the better chance she'll have.'

'Here, I say, old lad. You're not suggesting that Algy leaves us standing on this bally crust, or whatever it is?' said Bertie in a horrified voice.

'If we step out we're liable to go straight through,' asserted Ginger.

'Just a minute, don't get so excited,' snapped Biggles. 'Nothing much has happened yet, and nothing may happen. I'll get out first to test the ground.'

'Don't be a fool,' protested Algy.

'Don't worry. I'll take a rifle in each hand. If my legs go through the rifles will catch on the moss and support me. If that happens you'll have to haul me back and we'll try something else. The idea isn't original. In bog countries people walk about with a plank for the same purpose that I, not having a plank, am using the rifles. If the crust supports me – okay. The others will follow. Keep a fair distance apart. We'll make for the rising ground in front of us, where the rocks start. That's the end of the bog.'

'What about me?' demanded Algy, with some concern.

'You'll be all right,' declared Biggles confidently. 'Even if your wheels break through the wings will support the hull. Your job is to get off and fetch the Norwegians – but you'll have to find another place to land when you come back. I'll get out now. Sit still, the rest of you.'

The others watched while Biggles opened the escape hatch. Then, taking a rifle in each hand, and holding them as far away from his body as possible, he stepped out. His feet sank into the moss; black water oozed up round them, and the immediate area sagged a little under his weight – that was all.

'Okay!' he called. 'I think it's all right.' He thrust one of the rifles back into the cabin, and holding the other at right angles from his body he started walking slowly towards the nearest rocks, about a hundred paces distant. Slight as the movement was, it was sufficient to set the whole bog rocking again. Tense with suspense those in the aircraft continued to watch, watching while Biggles, maintaining an even pace, not even hurrying when he was near the rocks, made the passage.

Pent-up breath escaped from those in the aircraft when Biggles jumped to show that he was on firm ground. He sat on the nearest rock and waved.

'My godfathers!' exclaimed Bertie. 'What a bally nightmare. I'll go next.' Adjusting his monocle and taking a rifle he walked slowly to the rock where Biggles was waiting, smoking a cigarette.

Ginger followed. A few yards from the firm ground his impatience overcame caution and he made a rush for safety. Instantly his feet went through the scum and he found himself standing waist deep in coal-black mud. The others hauled him in.

'You dirty fellow,' said Bertie, wrinkling his nose. 'By gad! How the stuff stinks.'

'I thought I was going to be sick,' explained Ginger. 'That bouncing feeling got me in the stomach.' He wiped his forehead.

Biggles faced the aircraft and waved to Algy to take off. 'Von Schonbeck must have heard the machine land,' he told the others. 'If he sees it take off again maybe he'll think we're all away.'

There was no talking while Algy took off. For fifty yards the machine rocked as though it was riding an ocean swell; then Biggles drew a deep breath. 'It's all right,' he murmured. 'He'll make it. He's practically airborne.'

A few seconds later daylight appeared under the *Tarpon*'s wheels. Algy climbed a little way, and then, turning, headed back for the cove.

'We're well out of that,' observed Biggles. 'Let's see what von Schonbeck is doing.' Walking fast he struck off on a course which, he explained, he hoped would cut across the Nazis' path before they could reach the comparative safety of the hills.

After five minutes' sharp walking, from the top of a rise the Nazi party came into view, less than a quarter of a mile away, still making for the pass. Progress was slow, for four of the men were staggering under a heavy weight.

'He's had to abandon most of the gold, but he's hanging on to as much as he can move,' observed Biggles. 'He can't bear to let it go. The gold bug must have bitten him badly, as it's bitten others. Well, he'll see where it will get him. Come on.'

The party now moved forward at the double, still taking a line that would cut off von Schonbeck from the hills. And this, curiously enough, was achieved before they were seen – or, at any rate, before von Schonbeck, perceiving his danger, took steps to prevent it. A shot rang out and a bullet zipped through the scrub near Biggles's feet. He dropped flat, motioning the others to do the same. 'This will do,' he said.

The Nazis had by this time taken cover, so that they could not be seen, but their position was revealed by some loud talking. In particular, von Schonbeck's voice could be heard, pitched high.

'I fancy he's having a job to hold his men together,' remarked Biggles.

A moment later three men broke cover and ran as if to take up fresh positions outflanking the attackers. Biggles fired. The man at whom he aimed stumbled and pitched forward on his face. Bertie and Ginger fired together, apparently at the same man. He fell. The survivor of this futile counter-attack, bending low and swerving, ran back. Biggles fired and missed.

'They won't try that again,' he observed. 'Two down… that leaves four. Apparently von Schonbeck intends to fight it to a finish. Well, that suits me.'

There was now a period of calm. Biggles worked his way forward a little, as did the others, to close the distance; but the Nazis were behind cover and could not be seen. Four bullion boxes had been stacked together, and Biggles suspected that the Nazis were behind them. Refusing to risk casualties by a frontal attack he began to creep towards a new position from which the boxes could be enfiladed, but by the time he had reached it twilight had dimmed the scene, and all that could be seen distinctly was the silhouette of the mountains against the sky. The rest of the world lay in shadow, vague, menacing, lonely. Somewhere in the distance a bird wailed. A salt wind, bitterly cold, sighed across the dismal moorland.

Presently, on this breeze, came a drone, a drone that grew swiftly stronger.

'Here comes Algy,' said Ginger.

'Goodness knows where he'll get down,' answered Biggles, looking worried. 'This is a tricky place at any time, but in this light I'm afraid it's asking for it. But there's nothing else for it.'

The aircraft came on, and presently it could be seen, flying low. The bog, apparently, was Algy's landmark, for he flew straight to it, and then came on to sweep low over the scene of operations. Whether or not Algy saw the opposing parties on the ground, was not, at this juncture, apparent. It turned out subsequently that he did not. Biggles dare not risk standing up for this would have meant exposing himself to the enemy's fire. However, Algy went on, and after circling once or twice went down. His engines cut out and the aircraft merged into the colourless background.

The others listened, trusting to their ears to tell them what their eyes could not. Every sound of an aircraft landing was of course familiar to them. They heard the hum of the wind over the lifting surfaces. Then came a sharp, vicious thud.

'He's hit a rock,' said Biggles in a hard voice.

Another moment of silence came, then a harsh, splintering crash.

'I was afraid he'd got it,' said Biggles evenly. 'Listen. We shall soon know how bad it is.'

Voices could now be heard, perhaps a quarter of a mile away – perhaps a mile. It was hard to judge distance. Biggles moved to a higher point and strained his eyes in the hope of making out the shape of the *Tarpon*, but in vain. The background was too broken up by rock. There was more talking, then a voice called an order sharply.

'That was Algy's voice' declared Ginger.

'I don't think the crash could have been very serious,' said Biggles. 'They were too low – just gliding in.

Somehow we've got to make contact. We must let them know where we are or they may open up on us.'

'How can we make contact?' asked Ginger. 'The Nazis are between us. If we try to by-pass them it will be pitch dark before we get in touch with Algy.'

'There's only one way,' replied Biggles. 'We'll start the ball rolling. You and Bertie open up a brisk fire on those gold boxes while I move forward. Then I'll open up and cover you while you join me. Let's go. I'm getting cold.'

In accordance with this plan of attack Ginger and Bertie started firing at the gold boxes, the outlines of which could still be seen. Biggles dashed forward. There was answering fire from the boxes, but he ran fifty yards before he dropped, and bringing his rifle into action brought a quick fire to bear on the enemy's position. Bertie and Ginger appeared beside him. By this time weapons were flashing at several points.

'I think Algy has got the hang of it,' declared Biggles. 'He's got his fellows advancing, too.' Cupping his hands round his mouth he shouted, 'Algy! Can you hear me?'

An answering shout game across the solitude.

'Keep moving forward!' shouted Biggles. 'Close in on the boxes. They're straight ahead of you.'

For perhaps five minutes a minor battle raged, apparently without casualties on either side. Biggles and his party continued to advance in short rushes. Algy and his Norwegians did the same. Then, when they were within a hundred yards of their objective, the end came quickly.

A man sprang up from behind the gold boxes, and with his hands held high ran towards Biggles shouting 'Kamerad!' He did not get far. Another figure rose up behind him. A pistol flashed, and the would-be prisoner sprawled headlong.

'Nazis usually end by shooting each other,' said Biggles.

'Look out!' exclaimed Ginger sharply.

The man who had fired the last shot, instead of dropping back to cover had dashed forward. Bending low he continued to run. His figure and his peaked cap revealed his identity. It was von Schonbeck. He did not run towards either of the attacking parties, but went out towards the flank between them, as if concerned only with escape. Biggles sprang up and ran too, firing an occasional shot as he ran.

'Be careful!' yelled Ginger. 'That's the direction of the bog.'

Biggles knew it. He also had good reason to suppose that the Nazi did not know what he was heading for. He shouted to him to stop, not once but several times. Von Schonbeck's only answer was to turn and fire a shot from his pistol before going on.

Biggles followed. He was perhaps fifty yards behind von Schonbeck when the German reached the bog. He shouted a warning, dire and imperative, but the German ran on, with the ground under his feet beginning to rock with a long, ominous swell.

Biggles raced to the edge of the bog and then stopped. He shouted a final warning. Whether the German heard it or not, or whether, having heard it, decided to ignore it, will never be known. But he must have realised his danger, for instead of running in a straight line he began to swerve, as if seeking firmer ground. Once he turned and, poised unsteadily, fired another shot. Biggles returned it. Both missed. Von Schonbeck went on, running hard, dodging as he ran, presumably to escape the shots he thought might follow him.

In the end it was this method of retreat that destroyed him – or so it seemed to Biggles, who stood watching. Biggles was just beginning to get anxious, fearing that his man would reach the other side after all, when the Nazi, in making a swerve, stumbled and fell. There was a horrid sort of *plop*, something between a thud and a splash. Von Schonbeck did not rise. Where he had fallen appeared a black stain. It quivered for a little while, then settled down. The Nazi did not reappear. Silence settled on the scene.

Biggles pocketed his pistol and was tapping a cigarette on the back of his hand when Bertie and Ginger joined him.

Ginger stared out over the morass. 'Where is he?' he asked breathlessly.

'He's had it,' answered Biggles laconically, dropping into service slang. He pointed to the ominous stain. 'That's where he went through. Maybe it was the best way. It saves us the trouble of taking him home and saves the country the expense of a trial.'

Algy, Axel and the Norwegians came up to report that there were two dead Germans lying behind the gold boxes.

'Then that seems to be the lot,' observed Biggles. 'There's no longer any need for hurry. It's all over.'

CHAPTER XVIII

The End of the Trail

Algy jerked an apologetic thumb in the direction of the crashed *Tarpon*. 'Sorry I made a mucker of it,' he said moodily. 'I was in a hurry to get down. There was a place where I thought I could get in between some rocks, but I was wrong. I hit a lump at the end of my run and she tipped up on her nose. No one was hurt.'

'I wouldn't worry too much about that,' replied Biggles. 'It means that we shall have to walk home, and we had that in front of us, anyway – unless we were prepared to risk a night take-off and landing. It's... Hello! What the...!' He swung round as from near at hand suddenly burst the roar of a high-powered aircraft.

'A Nimrod!' cried Ginger in astonishment. 'What the deuce!'

'A Nimrod usually means there's an aircraft carrier in the offing,' said Biggles.

'Here, I say, by Jove! There's another!' exclaimed Bertie, dropping his monocle and catching it deftly in his left hand.

'It looks as if Raymond has decided to take a hand,' surmised Biggles.

'Trust reinforcements to roll up when the show's all over,' said Ginger, a trifle bitterly.

'I wouldn't say that,' reproved Biggles. 'Raymond wasn't long getting on the job, you must admit, when we told him we needed help. Apart from that I'm relieved to know that we shan't be marooned on Kerguelen. I, for one, have seen enough of it.'

'Absolutely, old boy, absolutely,' murmured Bertie. 'Beastly place.'

'That Nimrod pilot has spotted us, but he has too much sense to try putting his kite down in this wilderness,' remarked Biggles, watching the nearest machine which, after circling overhead, made off in the direction of the cove. 'We'd better start walking,' he added.

'What about the bally gold?' inquired Bertie.

'Unless you feel like carrying it, it can remain where it is for the time being,' returned Biggles. 'There's nothing on the island likely to touch it. Let's get cracking.' He struck off at a steady pace in the direction of the cove.

It was a cold, hungry, weary party which, some-time before midnight, plodded back to the starting-point, although it must be admitted that the last few miles were shortened by the appearance of bright lights in the vicinity of the cove. While some distance from the beach, the superstructure of a tall ship, anchored just outside the entrance, became visible.

'It's a carrier all right,' declared Ginger. 'There she is.'

'Looks like the *Vega*,' said Biggles. 'She must have been lying somewhere handy to get here in such a short time.'

A figure moved forward out of the shadows. 'Quite right, Bigglesworth,' confirmed a voice – Air Commodore Raymond's voice. 'You didn't suppose I was abandoning you in these God-forsaken seas, did you?'

'I didn't even think about it,' replied Biggles. 'I was too busy looking for what I came here to find.'

'And you've found it, I see,' observed the Air Commodore, inclining his head towards the shattered U-boat.

'Yes, we found it,' agreed Biggles.

'Where's von Schonbeck?'

'He's somewhere between the top and bottom of a bog of unknown depth about twelve miles inland,' informed Biggles. 'I doubt if it's worth looking for him. Some of his men are lying about though, so you'd better send out a working party in the morning to tidy the place up.'

'And the gold?' There was more than a trace of anxiety in the Air Commodore's voice as he asked the question.

'That's kicking about, too,' announced Biggles. 'It's all yours.'

Raymond smiled. 'So you don't want it, eh?'

Biggles shook his head. 'All I want is a bath and a bed.'

The Air Commodore laughed softly. 'No doubt that can be arranged. Come aboard,' he invited, and walked towards a motor-boat, manned by naval ratings, that waited near at hand. 'You'll be able to tell me all about it before you go to bed, I hope?' went on the Air Commodore anxiously. 'A lot of people at home are waiting to hear the story.'

'I'll see how I feel when I've had my bath,' answered Biggles non-committally as the party filed into the boat.

Except for the inevitable official inquiry that was the end of what Biggles afterwards called 'their second case'. With their Norwegian allies they returned home on the *Vega*, an easy, restful trip that occupied the best part of a month. Long before the carrier reached home waters

Biggles had rendered a full report, with the result that much to his displeasure the newspapers had got hold of the story, and with no war news to occupy their columns had put it on the front page. The names of the officers concerned, however, were at Biggles's request, omitted.

'We've had all we want of von Schonbeck and his gang,' he told Air Commodore Raymond, the first morning they reported for duty at their Scotland Yard office. 'As far as we're concerned it's all washed up. Think of something new.'

'I might even be able to do that,' answered the Air Commodore slyly.

'But not today, I hope?' put in Biggles coldly.

'All right – we'll leave it until tomorrow.' The Air Commodore went out, laughing.